THE KEEPER OF THE STONES

THE KEEPER OF THE STONES

Roz Kay

Illustrated by Kelsea Rothaus

HAYLOFT PUBLISHING LTD

First published by Hayloft Publishing Ltd., 2020

A CIP catalogue record for this book is available from the British Library

ISBN 978-1-910237-58-8

Designed, printed and bound in the EU

Hayloft policy is to use papers that are natural, renewable and recyclable products and
made from wood grown in sustainable forests. The logging and manufacturing processes
are expected to conform to the environmental regulations of the country of origin.

Climate neutral
Print product
ClimatePartner.com/12667-2002-1002

This book was printed with the offset of carbon emissions and support for
Forest Protection in Pará, Brazil.

Hayloft Publishing Ltd,
a company registered in England number 4802586
2 Staveley Mill Yard, Staveley, Kendal, LA8 9LR (registered office)
L'Ancien Presbytère, 21460 Corsaint, France (editorial office)

Email: books@hayloft.eu
Tel: 07971 352473
www.hayloft.eu

To Josie and Nathaniel

Contents

A Herd of Bulls

Hundreds of years ago, the legend said, a wild herd of bulls appeared from nowhere. Nobody knew where they came from, but the ancient stone circle on our farm became known as the Bull Stones.

And in front of me now was a herd of strange bulls out of nowhere.

The field with the Bull Stones was right at the southern edge of our farm. My brother and I had ridden there in the middle of the night, our horses forging through drifts of snow beneath the stars. The moonlight painted the countryside into a dream landscape, vivid and different, the shadows brushed on as softly as charcoal. Our farmhouse slept like a cat in the snow basin below us.

Above us on the hill, the Bull Stones poked up like a circle of broken teeth in the mouth of a giant, picked out by moonlight against the midnight sky.

And between our farm below and the stone circle above, the bulls gathered.

They linked together on the hillside and paced toward us, like a line of hunters closing in on their prey.

The lead bull raised its head as though it was sniffing the

night air. Could it smell us? The bulls adjusted their direction as if the leader had checked his sat nav and now they were heading straight for us, silent and purposeful in the snow, a dozen or more of them.

'Let's get out of here,' I said.

'Get a grip, Lizzie,' Daniel said, his tone telling me I was an idiot.

But really it was that I was twelve and he was fourteen and he thought that made him superior.

I bit my lower lip. Our horses fidgeted, knee-deep in the powdery snow, edging backwards. I ran my hand, stiff in its winter glove, down Free's arched, tense neck.

'There's something weird about those bulls,' I said. 'That one in front has metal tips on its horns.'

The metal tips glinted like bronze in the moonlight, halfway down the great curved horns. The bull raised its head again and the night was so quiet I could hear it snuffing the air. With a sick thump in my stomach, I got the impression it had no eyes. Just blind sockets.

Daniel seemed to change his mind, because without saying anything he turned his horse and set off to the other side of the hill. I followed. Clumps of woodland stretched out below us and the distant hoot of an owl reached me.

The Bull Stones were the reason we were here. Daniel had spent the summer helping volunteers at an archaeological dig on a buried village from thousands of years ago, close to our farm. He had a theory the Bull Stones were a midwinter moon calendar used by the long-gone villagers. It was the winter solstice, the longest night of the year, with the bright moon making everything grey and ebony and white. A good night to test his theory, he claimed.

We rounded the hill. But even after we could no longer see the bulls, my back prickled.

Out of the corner of my eye I caught a flicker of movement in the trees lower down the hill. A rapid glimpse that vanished before I could focus, leaving an impression of another horse, another rider.

I snapped my head round and strained to see through the dark tangled trunks below us. But the shadows cast by the moon sank deep, and I could make out nothing in the woods. Anyway, I couldn't believe anyone else would be crazy enough to be out here at midnight. I must have imagined it.

Daniel didn't appear to notice anything, so I didn't mention it. He was inspecting the fence that bordered the field.

'I don't understand how those bulls got in,' he was saying. 'The fence isn't broken anywhere, and there aren't any tracks in the snow. They're just here.'

'It's like that legend about the Bull Stones,' I said.

'Right,' Daniel said, but he shook his head at my foolishness. 'There'll be an explanation.'

We both knew the legend, since it was about the stone circle on our farm. The story was that in the seventeenth century a herd of bulls sprang out of the ground inside the circle. The villagers killed them, or so the legend said, and gave the Bull Stones their name.

We were still riding around the slopes of the hill. Now we were back in sight of the farm crouched in the distance, dark and silent. Where the bulls had been, there was only churned-up snow.

'See, they've gone,' Daniel said airily. 'So much for your legend. Let's get to the Bull Stones so I can check my theory.'

Him and his stupid theory. I glanced at the woods, wondering if the bulls had slipped in between the trees, wondering if I really had seen a stranger on a horse.

The next moment Free slammed herself sideways and I almost fell off. She bolted and Daniel's horse Molasses leapt after her. I tugged Free back under control and looked behind me.

The bulls were charging at us, fast and silent with the snow flashing up in fountains around them. Straight and true in our own tracks.

Sightless or not, they knew exactly where we were.

'They followed us!' I yelled, and kicked Free on — not that she needed any urging.

Our horses shot off down the slope in the direction of the farm, but the bulls flashed below and turned us like dogs rounding up a couple of escaping sheep. The next moment they were driving us up the hill towards the Bull Stones.

Free was faster than Molasses, and I looked back frantically for Daniel. I was afraid he'd fall. Dad said I rode like a Cossack, but Daniel rode like a book-reading, archaeology-obsessed geek. He sometimes joked he named his horse Molasses to help him stick in the saddle.

If Daniel fell off, he'd be in the path of the bulls.

'Hold the mane!' I yelled at him.

I saw him grab a handful of mane and reins and try to tug Molasses slower. But the bulls were too close, the horses too afraid.

Behind Daniel was the lead bull, the one with the bronze-tipped horns, gaining ground as it forged through the snow beneath a streaming cloud of its own breath.

Then I saw the other rider. Low on his horse, which was small and fast, a boy with a cloak. A cloak? He galloped straight up the hill to join us, shouting something and pointing at the Bull Stones.

It had to be the person I thought I'd seen in the trees, but now all I could think about was trying to get away from the bulls. A moment later the boy was alongside us, our three horses racing each other. We reached the top of the hill with the boy in front. Daniel was still clinging to Molasses, but he'd lost his balance and was tilting in the saddle.

The bulls were closing in, right in our tracks.

The boy in the cloak led us up to the Bull Stones, the great uneven blocks etched with moonlit shadow. He shouted something I didn't understand and galloped between the stones, waving at us to follow. We tore after him across the centre of the circle.

The moment I passed between the huge stones, a metallic ringing noise exploded in my ears. The moon flickered like an old black and white film, engulfing me in staccato light and darkness. I squeezed my eyes shut. The sound of a huge wind filled my ears, and the suffocating scent of snow blocked my senses.

Then everything stopped, including the horses. I opened my eyes and it was daylight.

How could it be daylight where moments before it had been the middle of a starry night?

I sat rigid on Free, utterly confused. Beside me Daniel was open-mouthed with amazement.

And beside him was the stranger, the boy in the cloak. Wild and dirty, silent, riding bareback. Even more of a Cossack than me.

The bulls had followed us but now they were streaming away, already far down the hill and moving across the snow as fast as a shoal of fish.

The sunlight bounced off the white slopes, hurting my eyes. My heart thumped against my ribs like a panicking rabbit. Had I fallen off? Banged my head?

Was I dead?

'What happened?' I said.

'No idea,' Daniel said. 'But it's the best thing that's ever happened to me.'

Not to me. To me, it was more like the worst.

2

A New Language

One thing I was sure about. I had to get home. I turned to ride back along the path we'd taken, back to where our farm was.

Only our farm wasn't there.

No farm. No fence around the field. No gate that we'd come through. No road that we rode along to reach the fields. Instead, below me was a vast untamed forest, spreading out far beyond the small copses and stands of oak and ash that I knew in our fields.

The landscape looked familiar, but different—as though someone had blindfolded me and spun me round, and now I didn't know which way I was facing.

Turning Free again, I realised that the Bull Stones themselves had changed. The Bull Stones were made up of a single big ring, with some of the stones missing, some lying down, nothing complete or defined.

Now, I saw far more stones. I could see three complete circles, the Stones upright, twice my height and perfectly spaced, with two smaller rings beside each other inside the large circle.

My heart was thudding hard enough to splinter my ribs and I choked back a tidal wave of panic that threatened to burst me apart.

I turned to the wild boy.

'What's going on?' I asked. 'Where are we?'

The boy didn't answer. For a moment he didn't even move. Then he pointed across the hills. In the fading afternoon light Daniel and I stared at buildings, small but lots of them, on top of another hill about half a mile away.

There shouldn't have been any buildings.

But there were buildings. And a fence ringing the hilltop, tiny red dots of fires inside, sheep's wool straggles of smoke clinging to the air, people moving about, a track down the hill.

'This isn't real,' I whispered.

What I meant was, this had better not be real.

'I know where we are,' Daniel said. He was babbling with excitement. 'I know where this is. That's the hill where the archaeologists found the Bronze Age village. It's the site where the dig is.'

'What village?' I said.

I knew he was talking about the dig he'd been volunteering at in the summer. But I didn't want to believe it.

'It's the Bronze Age village,' Daniel said. 'The Bull Stones aren't a calendar. They're a channel to another layer of time. We're still on our land but it's in the Bronze Age.'

My hands twisted in Free's mane. The stranger, the boy, waited patiently.

'How many years ago is that?' I said.

'About three thousand,' Daniel said. A broad grin lit his face.

'We can't be in the Bronze Age,' I said. 'Maybe the archaeologists are rebuilding the village and we didn't see it.'

I knew they weren't.

'So explain why it's daylight now when five minutes ago it was the middle of the night,' Daniel said.

'You explain it,' I said. 'I'm not the explainer.'

'I just did,' he said impatiently.

I stared at the wild boy's horse, its bridle. Simple leather, decorated, and a bit through the horse's mouth that looked like my own horse's snaffle bit. Did they really have those three thousand years ago?

And his clothes. The cloak. A curly metal cloak pin glinted in the sunlight.

Daniel was still grinning like someone who's won the lottery. I closed my eyes and counted to three.

When I opened them again, I told myself, I'd either be in bed waking up from a nightmare or back in our fields in the moonlight. Even being chased by bulls with sightless eyes was better than this.

But when I looked about again, I was still there, in the late afternoon of a day that Daniel said was three thousand years ago. The boy was still with us, dirty and greasy. And with the breeze coming my way, he was totally stinky.

'Who are you?' Daniel asked him.

The boy frowned and turned to me, so I repeated the question. He studied us for a moment and then pointed to himself.

'Wightes clepen Tirvold.'

'That's his name,' I said, before I even realised I was going to speak. 'He's called Tirvold.'

Daniel's face turned red. I hadn't seen him this excited in years.

'I'm Daniel, and this is Lizzie,' he said.

The boy Tirvold ignored Daniel and studied me, and I scowled back. How did I know what he'd said? My confusion grew as I realised this boy (a boy from the Bronze Age, if Daniel was right) resembled Daniel. They had the same narrow face, straight thin nose and pointed chin, black hair and dark blue eyes with straight eyebrows.

My face was that shape too, but my hair was red and my eyes brown, and I had a lot of freckles.

'Yow allen nedeth fallowen,' Tirvold said. He pointed at the buildings again. 'To mae tonah.'

'Mae tonah?' Daniel repeated.

He was obviously mystified, but the words shifted in my brain and fell into place.

I knew what Tirvold was saying.

'He said it's his home,' I said. 'He wants us to follow him.'

'How do you know?' Daniel said, astonished.

'I don't know.' My stomach was churning, my hands clammy with sweat inside my gloves. 'It feels right.'

Tirvold rode away. After staring at each other for a moment, Daniel and I followed. There didn't seem to be anything else we could do.

I'm going to wake up any moment, I thought. I'll see the pictures lit by moonlight on the walls in my room, check my mobile for messages, snuggle up again under my duvet with my cat Molly...

Except I was riding on a winter afternoon, following a stranger in a cloak, three thousand years before I was born.

3

The Horse People

We rode to the village, staying close behind Tirvol. 'Where did the bulls go?' Daniel asked him.

Tirvold glanced back at us and frowned. He seemed to frown a lot.

'The bulls?' I repeated. 'Where are the bulls?'

When I spoke, the words changed in my mind. What came out sounded like my own words to me, but Tirvold seemed to understand me although he hadn't understood Daniel.

'Boles,' Tirvold said, nodding. 'Arte runnen, ech dan oother, a Longen Moonde. Ther lyven alongen Bole Mester.'

'I wish I knew what he's saying,' Daniel said, sounding frustrated. 'Or even what language it is.'

I was silent, concentrating on Tirvold's words repeating themselves in my mind. They dropped into place as softly as dancers falling into line.

'He said the bulls ran into the Long Mound with the Bullmaster,' I said.

Daniel stared at me. 'You what?' he said. 'You're not telling me you understand him.'

I did, but translating didn't help much.

'I don't know what he's talking about,' I said. 'It's just words in my head.'

Daniel thought for a moment. 'The Long Mound is where the archaeologists found the buried warriors,' he said.

'Apparently, it doubles as a cattle shed,' I said sarcastically.

Daniel laughed, making me hope again that he was playing some elaborate trick on me. Then he stopped laughing and frowned, more like Tirvold than ever.

'How do you know what he's saying?' he said. 'When you repeat it, it sounds right, but I don't get what he's saying at all. And when you spoke to him, you sounded like him. I didn't understand you either.'

I was as bewildered as he was. And a lot more scared.

'I don't know,' I said. 'When he talks, I don't know what he's saying right away. Then the words trickle about and I understand them.'

It was like a picture that was out of focus, so all I could see were the colours. And then something shifted, and it came into focus and I could see the shapes. Except it was words, not pictures, and I heard it in my head instead of seeing it.

Daniel didn't reply. He didn't seem too happy I could do something he couldn't.

Flocks of small, scraggy, long-tailed sheep and thin tatty goats were nibbling at the grass beneath the snow, and further off I saw several herds of loose horses. I picked up a lock of Free's silky black mane, twirled it round a finger, dropped it, started again. This had to be a dream.

But as dreams went, it was starting to feel too long.

And much too real.

4

Rugal

People thronged in the gateway as we arrived, jostling each other to get a better view of us. Like Tirvold, the men wore caps and tunics, long cloaks in muted but wide-ranging colours woven into checks and stripes, and heavy sheepskin boots.

One man strode in front of the others, his cloak swinging open over a leather scabbard topped by a sword hilt. The rest followed him and we were surrounded.

A stench rose from the men that almost overpowered me. No hot showers here.

'Onkel,' Tirvold said.

He tipped his chin towards the man. His uncle had greying hair, a heavy beard, and pale grey eyes as hard as concrete in a set, lined face.

A teenage boy, perhaps a couple of years older than me, rode up bareback alongside us, sitting his chestnut stallion as though they'd been foaled together. His curly hair was as red as his horse's. It hung down between his shoulder blades. Big gold earrings — Tirvold wore earrings too — flashed in his ears. Around his throat, some kind of a gold neck ring gleamed in the last of the sunlight. His horse wore a leather neck strap, ornamented with bronze discs and other shapes. The bridle was decorated too.

The boy's gaze locked with mine, and I looked down, feeling

my face turn hot. I studied my reins, smoothed Free's mane again, and tried to ignore the red-haired boy and focus on the scene around us.

A high bank of earth encircled the top of the hill, the fence on it made of rough wooden poles driven vertically into the earth, about a metre and a half high. The bank was about the same height. All the houses were inside the stockade.

Outside the stockade was a ditch, perhaps deeper than it appeared because it was half-filled with snow. A narrow earth causeway crossed it and led to the gateway.

Some women were joining the men. The people, maybe thirty of them altogether, grouped themselves on the causeway. Their voices—questioning, astonished—drifted over.

I caught some of the words 'Seeyen clothen tharenten...' which had to be 'see their clothes.'

I was wearing a scarlet puffy jacket with my jeans, and riding boots that I was wishing were warmer—all pretty standard, but high fashion for the Bronze Age, I was sure.

'Nae! Halten!' somebody shouted to a child running towards us. The words slid sideways in my head to become No! Stop!

Talk about a travelling show. We were the freaks. If I got my act together I'd be able to start charging them a fee to stare at us.

Out of the corner of my eye, I saw Tirvold riding toward us with his uncle and the red-haired teenager. Tirvold's thin face was steady, but his hands had a life of their own, his fingers working the reins anxiously. He pointed at the other two, making introductions.

'Clynwas, mae onkel,' he said. 'Rugal, mae cosyn. Hors-eh

wightes aren uswe.'

He raised his eyebrows at me, apparently as I was now elected translator, to see if I understood. I nodded.

'Clynwas, your uncle,' I said. 'Rugal, your cousin. You are Horse People.'

Tirvold went on. 'Passen mae throw tha Ston-eh Circles dayen fif.' Daniel looked at me questioningly.

'He's saying he went through the Stone Circles, what we call the Bull Stones, and was in our time for five days,' I said.

'That's how we did this?' Daniel said. 'That's the best thing I ever heard. I bet it's the moon. I always said the Bull Stones were linked to the moon. A moon calendar.'

'Some calendar,' I said. 'Flip a page and it's three thousand years different.'

But Daniel didn't care. He was too excited. I was not excited at all.

The rest of the men who'd accompanied Tirvold's uncle crept closer, all trying to get closer to us. Perhaps a dozen of them, tall and short. Some were bigger than Daniel. A couple were positively stumpy.

Their flat-cheeked faces were ruddy. They were farmers' faces. Like my own people, these people worked outdoors. They could have been my relatives, if you whisked them three thousand years forward and gave them a change of clothes and a haircut.

Up close, Rugal the red-haired cousin had eyes that shone green as glass beneath sand-coloured eyebrows. His skin was dense with coppery freckles and he had the same outdoor glow as the rest of them.

Rugal rode up to me, side-stepping his horse until we were

exactly in stride, controlling his stallion with inch-perfect preci-
sion. He stretched a hand across the gap between our two horses
and fingered Free's rein, then leant back to feel the edge of the
horse blanket I'd tossed across Free's back before we left.

'Nae drede,' he said, sitting forward again and smiling at me.

The words sharpened into focus in my head. No dread... do
not be afraid.

We all rode across the causeway. A few scrawny dogs ran
about, barking at us. The houses were just huts, mostly round,
built from wood poles and earth. Smoke rose from the tips of
the low conical roofs, which were partly covered with snow.

The path we were following had been laid with rough-hewn
wood, the horses thudding on the uneven boards, slipping sometimes on ice. Half-frozen manure and knobby rubbish crusted
the ground: bone pieces, broken pottery, ash and clinker from
people's fires.

A couple of times I saw small brown shapes slinking round
corners. Rats.

Rugal disappeared as a growing crowd followed us into the
village, and now they began cramming against us. A young
woman ran her hand down my jacket, and at once everybody else
was trying to touch me or stroke Free. They tugged at my saddle,
ran the leather bridle straps through their fingers.

Ahead of me Daniel was getting the same treatment. He
turned and grinned.

'I feel like a royal visitor,' he said.

I felt like a freak. Or these people were the freaks, touching
and poking at me.

A few goats, some sheep, and even a bony cow moved between the huts. One of the sheep disappeared, bleating, through a doorway into what I'd thought was a building for people. Maybe it was.

I remembered my mobile and took it from my jacket pocket. But it was dead, no reception. Mobiles didn't exist yet.

What else didn't exist? Airplanes, television, cars, radios. Plastic. Fridges. Electricity, bicycles, cookers, microwaves. I tried to stop myself, but my brain hit maximum speed, coming up with more and more things that weren't going to be invented for an awfully long time. Pens and pencils, movies, books, candles, matches, socks, watches…

I realised my eyes were closed, burned shut with tears I was trying to squeeze back, and I heard Daniel say, 'Lizzie, it's all right.'

I opened my eyes and took a deep breath.

'Can't we go home?' I asked.

'Soon,' Daniel said. 'But I don't want to go yet. Let's see what happens. I'll take care of you.'

Moments later, Rugal arrived on foot with a dog like a thin, brown foxhound at his heels. Tirvold dismounted and told us to do the same. Then Rugal gathered the reins of all three horses and led them away. My anxiety shot up—where was he taking Free?

We walked with Tirvold until he stopped at a hut like the others, low and round, with smoke rising from a central chimney. Although it wasn't so much a chimney as a hole in the conical roof.

Tirvold drew aside a broad cowhide hanging across the doorway like a curtain and ushered us in. The inside was one large round room, gloomy and smoky, a decent fire burning in the centre. Goats lounged near the flames, warming themselves. A large pottery jar containing water stood near the fire, and shelves fixed to the wall posts were stacked with clay beakers and wooden bowls. Firewood was piled by the doorway. Furs and sheepskins were heaped on a couple of plain wooden benches, and the floor was thick with dry grass and small twigs — not very clean. The place smelt of goats and smoke.

In the Bronze Age, this was our home.

5

The Bullmaster

When night fell, Tirvold took me and Daniel to the main square to share the village feast. The Horse People were cooking a couple of deer, spitted and whole, over a bonfire.

We sat on furs on the ground beneath a black sky frosted with the same stars that would still be shining on my family's farm in another three thousand years. The Horse People stood or sat in groups, men and women and children tearing off sizzling pieces of meat from the spitted animals and eating it in dripping chunks.

Tirvold disappeared, leaving us to eat.

'This is pretty tough,' Daniel said, stripping the last shreds of meat from a bone. 'But it tastes great.'

He tossed the bone to a dog, which grabbed it and ran off, pursued by a growling pack of its closest friends. He wiped his hands on his clothes.

'I'm going to look around for a few minutes,' he said. 'I'll be right back.'

I didn't want to be left alone but before I could object, he'd vanished. I hugged my knees in the firelight, surrounded by people who glanced at me occasionally, but seemed either too shy or too uninterested to approach.

One of the men was saying he'd given his grey mare to a travelling bronze-caster in exchange for an axe.

'It is a good axe,' he said grudgingly. 'But the mare was in foal to Rugal's fine stallion Sostis and I should have asked for some other thing too.'

I was beginning to realise this village lived and breathed horses, which made me feel a little more comfortable. Nobody who loved horses could be bad.

On the other side of the fire, Clynwas hacked off a hefty portion of deer and tossed it to his son, Tirvold's red-haired cousin Rugal. Rugal caught it one-handed, staggering as someone shoved him. A shout went up and a couple of the men jostled each other. It looked good-humoured—sort of.

Daniel reappeared out of the dark and smoke, accompanied by Tirvold, and they joined me again, tucking furs and skins under and around them for warmth.

I was wrapped in sheepskins and furs too. One seemed to be wolfskin, which made me anxious once more. Wolves. I tried to catch Daniel's eye, so I could remind him that we had to go home, but he was watching the tussle between the men. Five or six of them were still barging each other on the other side of the blaze, and the firelight glinted off daggers. Shouts leapt into the air with the sparks.

'Is that a fight?' I asked Tirvold.

Tirvold shrugged. 'Sometimes there is a dispute over who made the kill,' he said.

He gave a grin, jabbed his thumb into his leg.

'This part, the thigh, is the best. It's always for the hunter who delivered the death stroke. But sometimes we fight for it.'

Daniel frowned. 'I still don't get what he's saying,' he said to me. 'Do you?'

'Yes,' I said, astonished. 'It just sounds like English. You can't understand it?'

'Not really,' Daniel said. 'All that 'deeren' and 'nathena' stuff.'

'I heard English,' I said.

A warm glow spread through me, and it wasn't from the fire. For once I was ahead of Daniel in something, and I was going to make sure he knew it.

'I understand it all,' I said. 'Your A grades don't seem to help much here.'

Daniel didn't reply. He poked a branch in the fire and it cracked sharply, sending up a plume of sparks that died at once in the cold air.

'Why are we here?' I asked Tirvold.

'Come on, Lizzie,' Daniel said. 'Play fair. Now you're talking like him.' It set my stomach churning again.

'I'm not,' I said. 'I don't know what you mean.'

'When you talk to me, you sound like you always do,' Daniel said. 'When you talk to him, it sounds like him. The words are different. How are you doing it?'

'I don't know!' I said. 'It's not on purpose...'

My voice trailed away.

Tirvold was sitting with his knees up and his arms around them, like me — watching us. After a pause, he seemed to think we were ready for his explanation, because he started speaking.

'We are the Horse People,' he said. 'We breed great horses, and we train them. Rugal is a master trainer and so is his father, my uncle Clynwas. Our horses are known from far away, because they are strong and beautiful, and nobody can train horses like us. It is how we get gold, by training and selling horses that everyone wants, and our village is wealthy. So we have an enemy, and he is called the Bullmaster.'

'I can't understand any of this,' Daniel said.

'Shut up,' I said. 'I'll tell you later.'

I nodded at Tirvold and he picked up his story again.

The Horse People had a great queen, he said. The queen organised the village and made sure there was enough land for the horses. She was brave and strong, and she led the Horse People in battles to protect the land and the village.

'She rode without fear of man or bull,' Tirvold said. 'In battle, she struck off the Bullmaster's arm above the elbow with her sword, and she defeated him.'

He paused, and I stared into the heart of the bonfire, flames blue as ice on the blackening wood. How did it feel, to have someone smite your arm off with a sword? How did it feel to do it? Daniel sighed beside me, and I jabbed him quiet with my elbow.

'Did he die?' I asked Tirvold.

'We thought he died, but then the bulls appeared again, and we knew he did not,' Tirvold said. 'His arm is stone where once he had flesh. Some say that he died and this is his wight, for he shuns daylight and rides under cover of dark and lives deep in the Long Mound.'

Tirvold shifted his furs under him and lapsed into silence. I took advantage of the pause to fill Daniel in.

'What's a wight?' I asked him when I'd finished.

'Could be a man, could be a ghost,' Daniel said, as if it didn't matter either way. Always so reassuring, my brother.

Tirvold launched into his story again.

'Others say the Bullmaster hides because of his stone arm,' he said. 'Or because he has learnt magic but his powers are of the Moon, and wane by day but wax strong in the dark.'

Tirvold paused, and I explained the story to Daniel. He wanted to know about the magic—his calendar and the Bull Stones were on his mind. I turned back to Tirvold.

'What sort of magic?' I asked.

Magic that makes the Bullmaster strong, he said. Magic that he used to conquer people by terror and death. In villages nearby there were no women and no children. He sent in the bulls, and they took the women and children and drove them until they lay down in the snow and died. The men he kept alive, to work and fight for him.

But their souls belonged to the Bullmaster. They walked like the living dead and they took up arms for him. These were his army, men he had reduced to be like ash.

'This village, the Horse People's village, is almost the last one still fighting the Bullmaster,' Tirvold went on. 'If he defeats the Horse People and learns the secret magic of the Stones, his power will be complete, and many times greater than it is now.'

He stopped speaking and stared into the fire.

None of this sounded positive. Daniel was fidgeting. I asked Tirvold to wait, and updated Daniel

'Ask Tirvold about the bulls,' he said. 'Why can't they just kill them the way the kill deer?'

Tirvold shook his head vehemently.

'It is magic,' he said. 'They cannot be killed. The Bullmaster directs them.' Even talking about the bulls made him nervous. He looked beyond us into the dark, taking the tail of a wolfskin between his hands and twisting it as he talked.

A wolf seemed worse than a bull to me, but what did I know?

Tirvold said the bulls were dangerous at any time, but at night their power was far greater. When he passed through the Stones to our time, it was at night and the bulls were chasing him. They followed him into our time, but he arrived at dawn and was able to escape and hide himself and his horse. The bulls lingered in the top fields where they could conceal themselves in the woods. Nobody went there in the winter so nobody saw them, and nobody saw Tirvold either.

He came down the hill one evening to our farm, he said, and slept in the barn, although he didn't use the word barn. He called it the great building.

He dropped the wolf tail and smiled at me, amazement lighting up his face.

'I saw your horses there,' he said. 'It was light, and it was warm inside the great building. I saw metal creatures that made loud sounds and smoke, and carried you and your family.'

Our cars and Dad's tractors? He'd stolen food too. I told Daniel and he was delighted by this, delighted that Tirvold had found his way to our farm.

'Wait,' I said. 'That explains Mum blaming us for that loaf of bread disappearing.'

'Apples and ham too.' Daniel laughed so loudly that Tirvold grinned too, even though he didn't understand what we were saying when we spoke to each other.

Tirvold was looking at me expectantly, waiting for me to finish sharing his story with Daniel. We settled again.

'Go on,' I said to him.

6

Deep Magic

'Our people became rich, trading our horses for gold,' Tirvold said. 'Our queen had many horses, and her wealth grew.'

He paused as the bonfire crackled and flared, vermilion sparks flying upward as someone tossed on more branches. Coils of smoke floated across the sky, dimming the stars. The meat was reduced to gnawed bones, the object of snarling brawls between the dogs.

Tirvold shifted position, crossing his legs, and his voice edged into sadness.

'A coughing sickness arrived in the village,' he said. 'It came with the first snow of winter. First the little children died, and then the old people.'

The Horse People were ruled by queens. First their queen died from the coughing sickness, the queen who'd fought the Bullmaster and struck off his arm. Then her daughter became queen, but she died too. And the Bullmaster was closing in again.

'Tirvold's talking about a coughing sickness,' I said to Daniel. 'What do you think that is? It kills them.'

'Maybe flu?' Daniel said.

Tirvold produced a knife and a half-shaped piece of pine from under his cloak and furs, and busied himself carving a small wooden animal.

'I had to find a way,' he said. 'I fear the Horse People will be lost forever. And it is my place to find the answer, because I am of royal blood.'

'He's a prince,' I said to Daniel. 'Or a king. I don't know which.' Daniel leant forward.

'I'm so frustrated I can't understand him,' he said.

I waved him quiet again.

Turning the wooden animal in his hands as he whittled, Tirvold explained.

The first queen was his grandmother and her daughter, the second queen, was Tirvold's mother.

'Your mother died?' I said, and Tirvold nodded.

'Then last winter, a bull killed my father,' he said. 'But my sister is older than me, and together we are still here.'

Tirvold was an orphan. I told Daniel and we stared at each other, aghast. It wasn't something I even wanted to imagine. I pushed my fingers into the thick fur of my wolfskin for comfort.

'Now the Horse People have a new queen,' Tirvold continued. 'She is Eothal, my sister.'

But Eothal was in hiding. She had fallen ill with the coughing sickness. Tirvold and few trusted Horse People kept her hidden until she began to recover. But somehow the Bullmaster found out what was going on, and sent the bulls after her.

'The bulls found her, and she could not get away,' Tirvold said. 'The bronze-horn bull gored her. It was in her leg, and she was on her horse so she escaped, but a Bullwound is always a Death-wound.'

The bronze-horn bull. The one I'd seen on the hillside above the farm, the one with the bronze tips on its horns that snuffed the air because of its sightless eyes.

A Deathwound. I pictured the fight. Eothal, dark-haired and cloaked like Tirvold, in the snow on a red horse, sword against bull, the bull driving his bronze horn into her thigh. I shook the image from my mind.

Tirvold was silent for so long after that, busying himself with shaping the little wooden animal, that I thought he'd told us everything.

'Your sister, Queen Eothal,' I said.

It was a tough question, but I had to ask.

'Did she die too?'

'Not yet,' he said. 'She is alive. It was dawn and the bulls returned to the Long Mound. But she will die.'

I caught a fleeting expression on Tirvold's face, the stamp of burned-deep fear. He watched the flames for a moment. They were sinking, the cherry-red embers folding softly in on themselves but still giving off plenty of heat.

'Eothal is very ill from her wound,' Tirvold said. 'She cannot ride or walk, so she hides. Some of our people think it is time to accept the Bullmaster will win, and let him win so he spares us. But the greed feud is growing in our village. '

'What's a greed feud?' I asked.

Tirvold said something I couldn't follow about Rugal, his cousin, and horse training, and arguments over gold. The greed feud was a family fight over money, it seemed.

Then he went back to talking about the Bullmaster, which he obviously thought was the bigger problem.

'The Bullmaster smells blood in this village,' he said. 'It may be that he will bring death to all, and the greed feud will cease to matter.'

'What does the Bullmaster want?' I asked. 'Gold? Maybe you should give him gold.'

'And die or be slaves?' Tirvold's head jerked up. He sounded incredulous. 'That would be bad enough. But it is not that. He wants the secret of the Stone Circles. The deep magic.'

He shook his head, concentrating on the wooden shape in his hands. He carved a few more shavings from the little animal. I could see now what it was. A horse.

'Only our people with royal blood, such as Rugal and Eothal and me, know the Stone Circle opens a path to other times,' Tirvold said. And the Bullmaster had somehow found out too.

But although a few others knew there was something magic about the Stones, magic that could take you to different times, only Tirvold knew how the deep magic worked.

'I am the Keeper of the Stones,' he said.

His father had been the Keeper before him, and taught Tirvold. The Keepers knew the secret of how the Stones worked, how to take the path through time. It was trusted to them. They could only use the magic in time of great need and they could never reveal it to the enemies of the Horse People.

But if the Bullmaster caught Tirvold, he'd force the secret from him.

'I don't get it,' I asked. 'Why does it have to be a secret?'

Tirvold sighed.

'Because in the hands of the wrong person, an evil person, moving in time becomes a weapon,' he said. 'Just as I have brought you here to help me, he could bring weapons or people to help him. He would destroy us, as he has destroyed the weaker villages already. He would make himself all-powerful, with the rest of us his slaves. He would change the story of the world.'

Abruptly, as if he'd had enough of explaining things, Tirvold got up and left. The party was breaking up anyway so Daniel and I walked back to our hut through the frozen, smoky dark, and I filled him in on the rest Tirvold's story.

Tirvold was crazy if he thought we could help him.

I had to get Daniel to agree to us going home before we ended up dead.

The hut we slept in contained other teenagers, dogs, and several goats, which didn't seem to mind sharing with us as we found space on the floor and arranged sheepskins and filthy woollen blankets about ourselves.

'When do they invent central heating?' I said.

'They don't,' Daniel said. 'You have to wait for the Romans to arrive in a thousand years or so.'

'It will totally be worth the wait,' I said.

☙☙ ☙☙ ☙☙ ☙☙ ☙☙ ☙☙

I woke up deep into the night, my heart thudding from a fractured dream.

I'd seen Daniel, or I was Daniel, sliding down snow between black trees, their ugly branches clawing the sky. My feet were carrying me down a snowy track, flying round a bend, no wind, silent, not even cold, or too cold to know it.

Then I saw a man ahead in the snow, raising his arm. His arm made of stone.

7

The Boar Hunt

After breakfast—hard bread and goat's milk—Tirvold arrived.

'Today we hunt for wild boar,' he said.

This was totally not in my plan for the day.

Tirvold handed Daniel and me clothes like everyone else's, the heavy woollen garments of the Bronze Age. I wondered who'd worn mine before me, not to mention for how long. Somebody who'd died from the coughing sickness, perhaps.

The clothes stank, though I probably did anyway after sleeping on the floor with the goats. I pulled the clothes on over my sweatshirt and jeans, and discovered something so important that I stopped caring about the smell.

'These things are warm,' I exclaimed, twisting about to admire myself.

Wool and sheepskin boots, a linen tunic topped with a short-sleeved woollen one, a heavy shawl, and a cloak like the ones everyone else wore.

Tirvold showed me how to fasten the cloak with a cloverleaf-shaped bronze cloak pin. I slid a fingertip along the cloak pin once he'd done it up. Smooth shank, a curled decorative top. For some reason, I loved it.

Daniel had dressed in his Bronze Age clothing too. While the others weren't paying attention, he held his nose and winked at me. Next to Tirvold, they were hard to tell apart.

'You two could be twins,' I said. 'I can't believe how much you look like each other.'

℮℈ ℮℈ ℮℈ ℮℈ ℮℈ ℮℈

The day had the dullness of pewter and the sky pressed on us, so low I could almost have touched it just by standing on my toes, reaching up. Even the cloak couldn't prevent a thin wind knifing its way in and raising goose bumps. I was grateful to be riding; it warmed me up.

Most of the hunters rode, though a few were on foot. Some of them caught their mounts from among the loose horses hanging around the village. They rode bareback or with woven blankets tied on like saddle pads, using simple leather bridles with bronze bits. Many of them had harness decorations, bronze discs and loops, cheek pieces carved from bone and antlers.

Everyone had bows slung over a shoulder, arrows strapped to their backs, a short spear in one hand.

A group of us, including Tirvold, Rugal, and his father Clynwas, rode down the track from the village and then cut left around the hill, heading south. I was unnerved by Clynwas, a hatchet-faced, silent man who avoided my eyes but stared at me when he thought I wouldn't notice.

I told myself it was my red hair. Daniel looked like Tirvold, but Rugal and I could have been brother and sister too.

Daniel was silent, tense and excited on Molasses. His clothing matched the other men and teenagers with their round caps and woollen cloaks. But the Horse People rode with just cloth pads and no stirrups, whereas we had our saddles.

Off to the right loomed a low, snow-covered hump, about thirty metres long and ten metres wide, although not more than two or three metres high.

'That must be the Long Mound,' I said to Daniel. 'Where the Bullmaster hangs out.'

'And where the archaeology team found those buried warriors,' Daniel said. 'Ask Tirvold how long it's been here.'

I did, and Tirvold gave it an uneasy glance.

'Always,' he said.

'Do the Horse People use it for burials?' Daniel asked.

I translated, or at least, I suppose that's what I was doing. In my own head the words sounded the same, but Tirvold and Daniel still couldn't understand each other.

Tirvold shook his head.

'Our ancestors did,' he said. 'But now we do not go near it.'

He tightened his reins, pushing his heel into his horse's side so that she side-stepped away from the Mound. Then he hurried us until we caught up with the others, and we slipped beneath the bare trees at the edge of a wood.

❧ ❧ ❧ ❧ ❧ ❧

Never in my life did I dream I would hunt wild boar on a crisp morning with the shouts of people who'd died thousands of years before I was born.

The hunters split into small groups and Tirvold went off with one of them. Rugal rode with me and Daniel. At one point, Rugal leant over from his red stallion and touched the back of my saddle.

'What do you call this?' he said.

'A saddle.' I indicated my feet. 'And these are stirrups.'

Those made an impression. Rugal studied them, his eyes narrowing.

'If you wore those in battle it would be hard for your enemy to tip you off your horse.'

'Yeah, that's what I've found,' I said.

His response to my attempt at ironic humour was an approving nod. He must have thought I really had been in battle. When I relayed the conversation to Daniel — who'd heard it but hadn't understood it — he almost fell off Molasses, laughing.

Finally, the hounds and lead riders entered a stretch of forest that seemed to be never-ending. Daniel and Tirvold followed but I hung back, not wanting to get lost, not wanting to be hunting boar at all. Rugal turned back towards me.

'Come with me,' he said. 'I will make sure you are safe.'

Relieved someone was looking out for me, I followed him beneath the trees.

The branches made imprisoning arms, a black lattice against the dove-coloured sky, a net closing in on me.

At first there was barking, but then the sound of the dogs died away. In the forest, the snow was light and powdery, the ground brittle with frozen puddles. There were no fallen branches or logs, and it occurred to me that the Horse People might get wood from here for their fires. Birds flickered through the twigs in huge numbers, and a blackbird broke cover, its alarm call ringing through the sharp cold air.

Rugal halted his horse.

'Wait here,' he said. 'I am not sure where they went. I will come back for you.'

People were always telling me to wait and then leaving me alone. Rugal sent his horse into the trees before I had time to protest. He vanished almost at once, but for a minute or two the sounds of his progress drifted back to me. A very long way off, a hound bayed. After that, I heard only winter woodland noises. Bird calls, the crackle of something moving in the deeper forest.

Closer. Behind me.

I turned Free, and she reared.

Even as I dealt with the rear, I took in the boar, and I screamed. I had no idea boars grew so flipping big.

Jaws snapping, tusks flashing, hooves stamping the snow.

And then squealing and charging, with somebody's arrow embedded in its dark, bucking shoulders. Free bolted into the forest and I bent low over her neck, urging her on, making myself as small as possible on her back as we fled beneath the trees.

The boar tore after us.

We might have outrun it, but the ground was pitted with holes and Free fell, pitching fast onto her knees. I flew over her head, my shoulder and hip slamming into the hard wet ground. Free was up in a moment and galloped off.

Leaving me winded and stunned. Wrapped in a red haze.

The boar was coming. Lying with one ear on the ground, I heard its hooves thundering.

I couldn't breathe. Lay there. Trying to suck air into my lungs. A strange whooping noise bursting from me. It was going to kill me and I was still winded, my fingers scrabbling at the frozen soil as I tried to get up. I made it onto on all fours, head hanging, still trying to catch a breath. And still the boar was coming.

I crawled to a tree trunk. Somehow, I dragged myself to my

feet and put the trunk between me and the boar as it charged, and it shot past me into a clearing. But it turned, throwing up a spout of snow like a skier. Its snout lifted, nostrils flaring.

Catching my scent. I reached up and grabbed branches, breathing in big sobs. My hip and my arm hurt, but I hardly noticed—I had to climb. So I climbed.

Three metres up the tree, with the boar churning up the ground beneath me, I clung to a branch, yelling for Daniel and swearing at him for getting me into this. Most of all, I wanted Dad with his shotgun.

A soft thunk made me look down.

The boar's legs splayed, an arrow in its neck. In the trees on the other side of the clearing, I saw Rugal's stallion Sostis, standing as though he was carved in red stone, with Rugal aiming another arrow. He let it fly and shot the boar through the eye. It crumpled against the tree trunk, showing its long yellowish tusks.

Rugal rode over the trampled snow to my tree. The boar was twitching, one hind leg kicking as it died.

'Lizzie?' Rugal called.

I slithered down, landing in an uncontrolled heap, my face in the snow. He was off his horse at once, kneeling beside me.

'Are you hurt?' he said.

I lifted my head and shook it. If I'd opened my mouth I'd have screamed and there was no way I was going to do that in front of Rugal. Baying, deep in the forest, reached us with the shouts of the hunters. The first of the hounds ran into the clearing as Rugal sat me back up and smiled, his eyes the polished light green of stones on a river bed.

'I want to wake up,' I moaned.

'Lizzie, you are awake,' he said softly. 'It is an amazing thing, to travel from your own time. A brave thing, braver for you than for your brother. You see more than your brother does, Lizzie Brave.'

The hounds began tugging at the dead boar, and Rugal left me to go and beat them off. They'd get their share later at the bonfire. Some of the other hunters arrived and Daniel was with them, riding Molasses and leading Free. He must have caught her somewhere.

I cranked myself onto my feet and limped over to him, taking Free's reins. I bent to feel her legs for bumps, to be sure she hadn't hurt herself when she fell.

'Are you all right?' Daniel asked, dismounting. 'It didn't get you, did it?'

'I'm fine,' I squeaked.

Then I took a deep breath and forced my real voice out.

'Being chased by a killer boar isn't that bad,' I said. 'You should try it.'

'So you're just wet through from lying about in the snow for no reason,' he said, and grinned at me.

I laughed at myself, a bit embarrassed.

'I fell off,' I said.

'Unbelievable—I didn't know you could fall off,' Daniel said. 'Next time I do, you won't be able to give me a hard time.'

He hugged me and I closed my eyes for a moment, relief surging back now my brother was here.

'You really are wet,' he said. 'Poor Lizzie. I know you're not getting as much of a kick out of this as me. Just give me one more day. I promise we'll go back.' And I believed him.

8

Kidnapped

Tirvold said he knew a shorter route back to the village, so we left the rest of the group dealing with the dead boar's transport arrangements. They were constructing some kind of a sledge from branches to drag it back to the village.

Our horses were tired but Tirvold chivvied us along, frequently checking the thickening sky behind us. He seemed as nervous as a cat that knows there's a strange dog in the room.

Snow began falling in huge soft feathers as dusk wrapped around us. The approaching night had a repressed, exhausted feel to it. A stinging little wind rustled over the snow.

For a short cut, it seemed to be taking a long time.

Daniel and I rode together, following Tirvold. I was too cold and hungry to care about much, except getting Daniel to agree to go home. We were arguing.

'We have to go back,' I said angrily.

'Lizzie, I know,' Daniel said. 'But not tonight. There's no moon—the sky's full of clouds. Don't we need a moon? Let's try tomorrow night. I can come back here anytime now we know how to operate it.'

'You're out of your mind,' I said.

But his face, even in the growing dark, was alight with excitement as we trotted along behind Tirvold.

'We can go forward, backward, anywhere,' he said. 'I can have two lives. I can live here. I can go back to our time and nobody would ever know I'd been gone.'

'What are you thinking,' I said. 'I could have been killed by that boar. You could be next.'

Daniel waved that away and told me his new theory.

'Time isn't a line,' he said. 'It's like a cake. Lots of layers you can cross into, all stacked up like layers of cake.'

Time layers. I could see that, the way the Bull Stones brought us here. I only hoped they'd take us back. My mouth was watering at the thought of cake and unless I was very much mistaken, there was no cake in the Bronze Age.

'I could live forever,' Daniel was saying. 'Each time I got old I could just go back to when I was young and start a new life somewhere else. The Bullmaster isn't the only one that can figure that out. It's the coolest thing ever.'

'Daniel, get a grip,' I said. 'We can't do that. You're crazy. Tirvold told us how many of them die or get killed.'

'Well, it wouldn't be the same for me,' Daniel said. 'If something went wrong I'd go back to my own time layer. I probably can't be killed.'

He grinned at me, all superior, and it made me furious.

'It doesn't work like that,' I said.

'How do you know?' Daniel said.

I was silent, remembering Tirvold's words about being the Keeper of the Stones.

'It doesn't feel right,' I said, but I couldn't have explained why not. Daniel slowed Molasses to a walk and I did the same with Free.

'Those archaeologists didn't find my body when they did all those excavations in the Long Mound, did they?' he asked.

I felt goose bumps running up my back, the imagined stabbing of bull's horns.

'That's not funny,' I said.

Daniel must have seen how disturbed I was, even in the dark. Or heard it in my voice.

'It's fine, Lizzie,' he said, but his voice was gentler. 'We'll go back tonight if we can.'

The wind was tearing holes in the cloud, letting the stars appear. I took a deep breath and sat up straighter in my saddle, feeling lightheaded.

'Thank you,' I said.

Tirvold halted and turned his horse, waiting for us at the night's edge. We'd almost reached him when Molasses stumbled and began limping. Daniel dismounted and lifted his horse's right front hoof. He cleared out the packed snow but when he led Molasses on again, he was still lame.

Tirvold slid off his horse too.

'It is not far to the village from here,' he said to me. 'Your brother must take my horse, Deer. She will carry him home. She knows the way. Night is coming and the wolves will be hunting soon. I will bring your brother's horse home slowly.'

I explained to Daniel. He looked dubiously at the blanket on Deer's back.

'Would she take my saddle?' he said.

Tirvold rejected the idea when I translated. He seemed more nervous than ever.

'Your brother will not need it,' he said. 'Deer will carry him safely.'

'What about the wolves and you?' I asked, trying not to let fear take me over completely.

'I have my bow and spear,' Tirvold said. 'When you get back to the village, ask my uncle Clynwas to send out a party to meet me with torches and weapons.'

Daniel was patting the blanket as if to make it more saddle-like.

'Shouldn't we all stay together?' I said to Tirvold.

Tirvold took charge of Molasses.

'No,' he said impatiently. 'It is more important for you to hurry back to where you will be safe and send the men to meet me. Go.'

Daniel heard the strain in his voice too, and clambered onto Deer's back.

'You must go,' Tirvold said. 'It is growing dark.'

With Daniel on Deer in the lead, my brother and I set off through the snow towards the village.

Glancing back, I saw Tirvold trailing us on foot. Molasses was limping along beside him willingly enough. Within a few seconds I could barely see them, even though the snow had almost stopped falling, as the shadows swallowed them up.

⚬⚬ ⚬⚬ ⚬⚬ ⚬⚬ ⚬⚬ ⚬⚬

The night wind tore up snow powder and flung it hissing across the plain.

Dark as jet against the snow, the bulls ran out of the gloom, turning me liquid with fear. We kicked the horses into flight. Racing the bulls. Racing each other. Free sprang past Deer and

I couldn't stop her.

I threw a glance over my shoulder. The bulls were closer, their ivory horns pricking the heavy sky as they gained on us.

But faster than the bulls was the cloaked figure that led them, bent low over his pale horse, shadow on snow, snow on shadow. Two bull horns — bronze or real, I couldn't tell — curved from his head. The Bullmaster.

He sat up on his galloping horse, raising his arm with an abrupt movement as some kind of direction to the bulls.

The gesture snagged something in my mind. I'd seen it before, but I couldn't remember where.

The bulls angled across the snow, running in a wedge. They were driving us now, cutting off the route to the village. I thought it might be possible to resist, to veer away, and yelled to Daniel to follow me, but he was struggling with his balance, not in control enough to steer.

No saddle, no stirrups to help him. I should have put him on Free and ridden Deer myself, but it was too late to think of that.

I hauled Free off the course the bulls had chosen and made her gallop a truer line to the village. I hoped Deer would follow, bringing Daniel. But she didn't, and the bulls abandoned me and went after him.

They drove him towards the sleeping hulk of the Long Mound.

Close behind Daniel was the Bullmaster, his big-striding horse overtaking Deer. I turned Free and started chasing them, but I was behind the bulls now and she was tiring fast, even with me kicking hard to keep her galloping.

In a slow, silent nightmare, I saw Daniel tumble into the snow.

My brother struggled to his hands and knees and then the Bullmaster was upon him, hardly easing up on his horse, reaching low and seizing Daniel, snatching him up like a dog, hauling him up across the horse's withers, sending the horse on again, pale horse over pale snow, dark sky, pale mound, straight at the Long Mound.

Straight at an opening in the end of the Mound.

Straight into the Mound.

Gone.

When I got there and leapt off Free, there was nothing but an unbroken wall of rock with tracks pouring into it.

I tore at the rock, screaming, Free backing away, and I found nothing beneath the snow but stone. I dug until my hands were numb, my nails broken, and my fingers bleeding, but it was rock, immovable.

Giving up, I ran to Free and flung myself onto her back. I galloped back the way we'd come, looking for Tirvold — but there was no sign of him.

So instead I fled to the village as fast as my exhausted horse could carry me. At the horse pen, I found Deer waiting. She'd made her way home by herself after Daniel fell off. I put them both in the pen with some armfuls of hay from the storage hut, and ran to the square.

Just like last night, everyone had gathered there. They'd dragged the boar back somehow — so much for our shortcut, or maybe time had warped — and several men were quartering it to roast the meat over the fire.

I couldn't believe it was all so normal. Tears streamed down my cheeks as I hunted desperately for Rugal. I found him laughing with friends near the fire. I grabbed his arm and he looked into my face, surprised.

'Please help me,' I said. 'The Bullmaster took Daniel. I can't get in the Mound. Tirvold's out there with the wolves and he needs Clynwas. Please help me.'

The response I got was shocking. A complete silence fell over the group. Then, talking in low voices, they all left. Except Rugal.

'Where are they going?' I said. 'Didn't they understand?'

'Yes, they understand,' Rugal said. 'They will look for Tirvold, but they can't help you. Your brother is not one of the Horse People. Rescuing him from the Bullmaster, if it is even possible, would mean many in our village die.'

'But you,' I said, letting go of his arm. 'You'll help me?'

Rugal hesitated.

'I will help you,' he said finally. 'But it cannot be while it is dark. It must wait until morning.'

9

Family

I snapped awake and jerked upright, a sob hitting the back of my throat. The hut was as dark and smelly as the inside of a fox den. I'd wrapped myself in Free's blanket and I had to bite the thick edge of it to stop myself crying out.

Whatever else I'd been afraid of in my life, the only fear I had room for now was never seeing my brother again. The fear was bigger than me — I was a crystal of ice in the middle of it.

The early light had the soft, clinging feel of charcoal powder. My tongue was sticking to the roof of my mouth and I groped for the water jar, dipped in a beaker and drank.

At least with the fire in the hut, as well as the warm bodies of people, dogs, and my friends the goats, the water wasn't frozen. But it was still cold enough to give me a brain freeze and my head started to throb.

Feeling washed out and ill, I crawled to the door-flap and got to my feet outside. It was lighter than in the hut, with the approaching dawn making the sky as hard and shiny as a seashell.

I trudged through fresh snow to the horse pen in search of Rugal. Deer was there. But Molasses was still missing, so Tirvold must be too. I slipped over the rough wooden rails and buried my face in Free's furry neck, breathing in her warm horse smell. For as long as I could remember, that smell had been my security blanket.

'Lizzie Brave,' a voice said.

It was Rugal. He was the only person anywhere, in any of Daniel's time layers, who thought of me as Lizzie Brave.

'Do you still want to ride to the Mound?' Rugal said.

I nodded.

He handed me a chunk of cold boar—breakfast.

'Come,' he said.

We readied the horses. As we set off with Rugal's dog jogging behind us, the sun hitched itself fully above the horizon, painting everything around us a pale saffron. The cold crouched tight over the land beneath the cloudless sky.

For a while we said nothing, but then Rugal spoke.

'So, Lizzie Brave, you have lost your brother.'

I was filled with a surge of anger against them all, especially Tirvold, but even Rugal.

'My name isn't Lizzie Brave,' I said sullenly. 'It's Lizzie Greenwood.'

Even in my preoccupied state, I noticed Rugal stiffen with surprise and felt the intensity of the look that followed. I glanced at him and thought I caught hostility in his expression, but then it was gone.

I must have offended him. If I had, he got over it quickly.

'Lizzie Brave is a good name for you,' he said firmly.

We rode on in silence, wrapped in the fog of our horses' breath. We ate as we rode, one-handed, tearing the boar meat with our teeth. I'd had nothing since breakfast yesterday, and I was appallingly hungry. The sick feeling in my stomach receded as each bite went down.

'Lizzie Greenwood,' Rugal said, wiping his sleeve across his mouth. 'How is it that you share Tirvold's family name?'

'What?' I stared at him. Now I knew what had surprised him, and it startled me too.

'Tirvold's family, the royal family, is of the Green Wood. And your name is Greenwood. Is it not the same?'

Daniel and Tirvold were close enough in appearance to be brothers, even twins. And I shared red hair with Rugal, as long and thick as his. If I was descended from Tirvold, I had a blood connection back through the centuries with Rugal too, since he was Tirvold's cousin.

Was it really possible that we were of the same bloodline, down through those thousands of years?

'My family's lived here as far back as we can trace,' I said.

'What does this mean?' Rugal said.

But I couldn't explain to Rugal, who had no notion of reading or writing, what it meant. How Daniel investigated our genealogical tree last summer when the history bug first gripped him, tracing Dad's family back to the early sixteen hundreds in the local parish records of births and deaths. Always farming or working on the land.   Give or take a couple of thousand years...

'Greenwood,' I said, taking another bite of boar meat. But I was full, and I threw the last piece to Rugal's dog. 'It sounds the same.'

If Tirvold was my direct ancestor, that would make me part of his royal family. And if I was descended from queens, did that make me a queen too? Daniel said he felt like royalty when we arrived at the village. If this was our family history, we really did have royal blood.

Rugal had a strange half-smile on his face.

'Maybe it is true you are one of the Horse People, and that is why you ride like one,' he said.

I sat straighter in the saddle, pride warming me.

We were close to where our farm would be built one day, the horses faltering now and then in unexpected pockets of deeper snow. In the Bronze Age time layer, the meadow was woodland and vast wild hedges. Birch, oak, beech, and pine ran across what would one day be our home meadow and apple orchard.

An explosion of frantic small birds—blue and great tits, robins, dunnocks, wrens—burst shrieking from the edge of the woods. A sparrow hawk arrowed across the snow, singling out a dunnock and seizing it in mid-air with a little puff of feathers.

'Does Tirvold know we have the same name?' I asked. 'He said he knew why the Stones had taken him to our time.'

Rugal concentrated on parting his horse's mane.

'Tirvold said this because Daniel looks like him,' he said. 'He went through the Stones and found Daniel, and saw him as someone he might pass off as himself. Someone he could give to the Bullmaster in his place.'

I bit my lip hard. What had Tirvold done? Rugal still wasn't looking at me.

'You mean it was a trick?' I said, my voice shaking. 'Why?'

'Because the Bullmaster wants the secret of using the Stone Circles,' Rugal said. 'It would give him great power. This is why he was trying to capture Tirvold, to learn it from him. But he would kill Tirvold too, so Tirvold will do anything to remain free.'

My heart was thudding so hard I was afraid my lungs would burst.

'Now what?' I said.

'The Bullmaster will make Daniel tell him how to use the

Stones,' Rugal said.

'Daniel doesn't know,' I said.

'You came together from your time,' Rugal said. 'He must know.'

Did he? I'd felt things as we passed through the Stones that Daniel didn't seem aware of, that had passed him by. I knew how the Moon and the Stones worked together, but I was increasingly sure my brother didn't.

'I don't think Daniel would understand the Bullmaster,' I said.

The language of the Horse People was clear to me, but not Daniel. Was that another part of the deep magic?

I wondered if Tirvold suspected that Daniel and I were his family. If he did, and he still gave Daniel to the Bullmaster, it was a betrayal.

'What do I do?' I said.

'We must look for the queen, Tirvold's sister Eothal,' Rugal said. 'I know where she hides, and Tirvold will be with her. Without Tirvold, you cannot get the Bullmaster to free Daniel.'

'When can we look for Eothal?' I said.

'Soon,' Rugal said.

I urged Free into a canter. The snow wasn't as deep on the slopes, and Rugal kept his horse alongside me. The dog had an easier time of it, running where the snow's crust gave him some footing.

I rode automatically, thinking through the relationships. Rugal was Tirvold's cousin. So Rugal's father, Clynwas, was also related to the queen. I remembered what Tirvold has said about the greed feud—about gold and the royal line.

Maybe the former queen, Emoral, had become rich on the

horse training carried out by Clynwas and Rugal.

So maybe this lay behind the greed-feud, Rugal's family and the Greenwoods contesting the royal heritage and its wealth.

And there was the other thing, that Tirvold was the Keeper of the Stones.

℮℮ ℮℮ ℮℮ ℮℮ ℮℮ ℮℮

The wind brought with it the glittery scent of snow and wet trees. We slowed to a walk and approached the forest boundary, the Mound looming in the distance. A couple of men from the village emerged from the bare thickets with horses hauling loads of wood. They lifted hands in greeting as we rode by. Rugal called out to them, waved.

It slammed home again that I was locked in the Bronze Age.

'Do you really think Tirvold meant the Bullmaster to capture Daniel?' I asked. Rugal appeared to consider it.

'You saw what happened,' he said. 'Daniel was wearing Tirvold's clothes, and you tell me he was riding Tirvold's horse.'

'But Tirvold couldn't have arranged for Molasses to go lame,' I said.

'Perhaps not,' Rugal said. 'It was a stroke of fortune for him. Tirvold sees opportunities and takes them.'

I couldn't stop the nervous twisting of my fingers in Free's mane. 'What will the Bullmaster do with Daniel?' I asked

'If Daniel does not reveal how to control the Stones to him, he will keep him until he does,' Rugal said.

'And if he tells him?' I asked.

'He will have what he needs,' Rugal said, 'and he will kill him.'

The Long Mound

Burials. Even if I could find a way into the Mound, how would I force myself through the terrible blackness full of dead people to look for Daniel?

I saw myself trapped inside the Mound, maybe for ever. What if I put my hand on something dead? On Daniel, dead?

For the first time, I jumped beyond the immediate fear and was hit by the pain of telling Mum and Dad. They'd think I'd gone crazy. Absolutely crazy.

Maybe I had.

⤫ ⤫ ⤫ ⤫ ⤫ ⤫

Rugal and I neared the Mound. A wide, churned track lay in the snow from the night before.

I unstuck my dry mouth. 'What if the bulls are here somewhere?'

'They are always around,' Rugal said. 'But this does not mean they will attack. They watch what we do. They guard him at all times.'

He tilted his chin toward the far end, where the tracks led.

'My grandmother said there is a way in over there,' he said. 'But it is blocked with stone doors that we call the Endstones. It is not possible to move them except by magic.'

I said nothing, wondering what either of us could possibly do to save Daniel.

We rode to the Endstones. The sun was bold in the winter sky and our shadows tracked us along the snow wall. It was hard to believe the Mound had opened up for the Bullmaster.

I dropped from Free's back into the snow, looping the reins round my arm, and inspected the area I'd cleared in my frenzied digging in the dark.

A narrow crack separated the two huge rock slabs. I hadn't found the crack the night before. Looking up, I saw the tops of the slabs were beyond my reach. They appeared permanent, immovable, but they'd been open last night for the Bullmaster.

'There has to be a way,' I said.

'Nobody knows how to move them,' Rugal said.

He was still on his horse.

'I'll find out,' I said, knowing it was hopeless.

Even in my desperation, I realised that breaking into the Mound while the Bullmaster was at home wasn't the best course of action.

Still, I put my mouth to the crack and called my brother's name.

Then I pressed my ear to the gap and listened, but there was nothing to hear. Frustrated, I banged my forehead against the cold wet rock and then clutched it. Not smart.

'There has to be a way,' I said again, rubbing my forehead. 'There has to be.'

Rugal sat silently on his horse. I took a deep breath and got a grip on myself. If there was another way, there was only me to think of it.

What would Daniel have done, if it had been the other way round—me in the Long Mound with him trying to get me out?

He'd said, We can go forward, backward, anywhere. I can have two lives.

'Oh, I'm so stupid!' I said. 'This isn't the way. I'll go back to before it happened. Then I can stop it.'

Rugal frowned. 'What do you mean?'

I remounted, warm with excitement.

'Let's go back to the village,' I said. 'Tonight I'm going through the Stones. Then I'll be able to change it all.'

❧ ❧ ❧ ❧ ❧ ❧

As evening fell, I took off the clothes I'd borrowed and left them folded on the floor of the hut, except for the cloak pin. It felt like stealing, but I wanted to keep it. The horse blankets I rolled up together to take with me, tying them with some Bronze Age cord.

If my plan worked, I wouldn't have to come back to this time layer. I checked around to make sure I hadn't left anything. The cloak pin was straight and strong in my jeans pocket.

As I left the hut in my puffy jacket, Rugal appeared. He looked me up and down, taking in my clothes and my excitement.

'You are going,' he said.

'Yes,' I said.

A surprising pang hit me. I was starting to think of Rugal as a friend.

'I want to come with you,' he said.

He shifted his bow and arrows on his back and gazed down

at me hopefully, only a few inches taller than me.

'You can't,' I said. 'I'm not coming back, if this works. I'm going to make sure Daniel and I never come here in the first place.'

There was a strange look on Rugal's face—desperation?

'I would come back on my own,' he said. 'You can show me how to do it.'

I remembered Tirvold's warning that the deep magic must be kept secret to protect the Stones from being used for evil. But I didn't need Tirvold's words. My blood vibrated in my veins, cautioning me.

I waited, silent, wondering what to do—but two of Rugal's friends appeared and dragged him off to the main square, and I rode out alone through the quiet village.

The snowstorm had blown itself out much earlier. The moon was rising and I didn't have much time to get to the Stones. I put Free into a canter, worrying about wolves and the bulls, worrying that I was making the wrong decision.

My plan was to arrive in time to stop us going through the Stones with Tirvold on that solstice night.

I tried not to think about what would happen if I got back earlier and Daniel was there, but I didn't remember, and we went through it all again anyway. Maybe I was already doing that, trapped in an endless time circle.

I reached the Stones.

The night was thickening and I dismounted to wait. I reached out and placed my hand against the icy cold rock beside me, one of the Bull Stones. Beneath my palm, the rock hummed and vibrated.

It knew me.

The moon floated upwards into a silken sky, the night relaxing in silver light on snow.

When the moon lined up with the tallest stone, what in my head I called the Moonstone, I ran the few steps across the snow into the other circle, pulling Free with me.

A huge wind blocked my senses again. Once more I felt or heard the ringing, the roar, the moon blurring through its changes.

Silence. I opened my eyes. I was home. But right away, I knew my plan was in trouble.

It was broad daylight.

And instead of being winter, it was the middle of summer.

Home Again

Our farm was there, the same as always. The Bull Stones
were how I knew them too, some leaning, some fallen, the
inner circles missing altogether.

But it felt like an August afternoon, and I guessed it was the
August before it all happened. I'd arrived home earlier than I'd
expected. It would be weird living through three or four months
a second time. Would I be doing everything again, and remembering it?

Maybe that was how déjà vu worked—you'd slipped between
time layers.

But at least I was safe, and it meant Daniel was safe. Now I
could stop the crazy midnight trip to the Bull Stones, stop him
being captured by the Bullmaster.

While I got my bearings, Free tore at the long green grass
around us, a Bronze Age hunger in her belly.

I surveyed the hill slopes, thinking I might see the summer's
excavations on the Horse People's village. Sure enough, small
figures were moving around between trenches on a gridded area.
It was a strange feeling, knowing I'd been there three thousand
years before.

The dig seemed bigger than I recalled, but then I'd never paid
it much attention.

Beyond it was the low green ridge of the Long Mound.

Daniel might be at the dig right now, volunteering with the archaeologists.

But I really needed a shower. I stripped off my jacket, mounted Free, and rode home in my filthy jeans and shirt.

The house was empty. The Land Rover was out and so was the tractor. I unsaddled Free and put her in the orchard field behind the house, leaving her saddle and other things by the gate. She couldn't believe her luck, getting all that grass when she was expecting midwinter.

But there was no Molasses, and that puzzled me until I remembered Daniel sometimes rode up to the dig. He must be there with his horse.

I let myself in at the back door and walked into the kitchen. The only sound was a bee zizzing at one of the windows. I opened it and let the bee out.

The silence of the house planted a seed of anxiety.

I wouldn't be one hundred per cent happy until I found Daniel, and I shouted for him, just in case. No response.

My mobile, I thought. I should text him. I dug into the pocket of my jeans where it had been sitting unused in the Bronze Age, but it was dead.

My cat Molly appeared in the kitchen and purred around my legs as I opened the fridge. I poured a glass of orange juice, so cold that it seared my throat and felt just great. Molly sniffed my leg with her fastidious cat nose. The need for a shower overwhelmed me. I smelt really bad after all those nights sleeping with goats and living in somebody else's dirty clothes.

But first I wanted to check the date so I went into the farm office, a small room off the kitchen where Dad did the accounts. We kept drugs and antibiotics for treating the animals in an old fridge in there too. Mum was a veterinary assistant, so we handled a lot of ailments and injuries ourselves to save money.

There was always a big two pages-per-day diary open on the desk.

I was right about the month. The date was the twenty-fifth of August, months before our midnight ride into the Bronze Age. I grinned. I'd be going back to school soon, and I'd earn top marks in everything without even trying because I'd secretly be repeating the work. That would show Daniel.

The diary contained the usual planning stuff, details on animal feed, who'd phoned during the day with what message, and so on. Dad had written P, Top Field, Bank which meant he was ploughing our two biggest fields. He'd be gone until almost dark, ten pm at this time of year.

Underneath his entry, in Mum's writing, were the words Land Rover, service 1 p.m.

I glanced at the clock. It was just after three. So she'd be in town, but probably back about six.

I headed upstairs.

My room felt different, familiar and not familiar, but then it probably was different back in August. Anyway I couldn't think about anything except smothering myself in soap and shampoo and shower gel and hot water.

I found my phone charger and plugged in my mobile. Then I dumped my backpack on the floor and grabbed a towel and some clean clothes, leggings and an over-sized tee shirt.

Dressing after the shower, I looked at the shirt for a moment, puzzled. It was one of my favourites and it was a lot more faded than I remembered, as though it was older.

I took the cloak pin from my jeans pocket and tucked it into the small pocket on the front of the tee shirt. I'd show it to Daniel, my brother the archaeologist, as proof that what I was telling him was real.

He'd want to know about time layers. How did they work? I pictured a book with millions of pages. The page was open on my time layer, but the other pages represented other time layers: the past and the future.

The trick was in knowing how to turn the page, how to step into another time layer.

And I'd learnt how to do that.

But my time layer didn't feel right.

What if Daniel wasn't here? How many time layers could be open at once?

I tried to slow down and give myself room to think.

Daniel would be here, I told myself. At any moment he could reappear, riding back from the dig. I'd explain it all to him. Daniel wouldn't be in the trapped in the Bronze Age time layer, because this time around, we wouldn't go there.

Right then.

I blow-dried my hair. Then I brushed my teeth for what felt like a year.

When I slotted my toothbrush back in the holder, I stared at it for a moment. Something was wrong. There was no other toothbrush — only mine.

Mum and Dad had their own bathroom, and I shared this one with Daniel. So his toothbrush should have been there.

But it wasn't.

An octopus of fear uncurled in my stomach.

I hurried along the landing to Daniel's room. Standing outside the closed door, fingering the old wooden panels, I waited for the octopus in my stomach to retreat. Then I took hold of the door handle.

Daniel's room always made me embarrassed about mine. He was so organised, everything put away, and I couldn't even begin to keep my room like that. Just getting to my bed involved an expedition with a compass if you were unfamiliar with the layout.

And Daniel had tons more stuff than me: game consoles and controllers, books, his laptop, clothes, a whole thing with Manchester United which I'd never understood — we lived in Wiltshire. A guitar. And everything was shelved, filed, boxed, hung up, stacked up, or in drawers. He even lined up his posters to be perfectly straight when he stuck them to his walls.

I opened the door, and the octopus in my stomach shot icy tentacles through the rest of me.

This wasn't Daniel's room.

This was a room I didn't even know we had in the house. It was done out like a spare bedroom with a neatly made bed, a strange bedside lamp, and a spotless carpet. A few empty hangers clattered from a hook on the back of the door as I swung it open.

No posters, no books, no games, no clothes, no guitar.

Absolutely no Daniel.

I backed out and shut the door. I stood motionless on the landing, my mind in turmoil. Had I entered the wrong room? Surely I'd have remembered if we had a spare bedroom. But we didn't have a spare room at all — the farmhouse only had three bedrooms. My room, Daniel's, and Mum and Dad's.

No way this was the wrong room. It could only be Daniel's.

I crept in again, but it was still a spare bedroom. Nothing in it had anything to do with my brother.

I bit my lower lip, puzzled and afraid.

Mum and Dad's bedroom, which was next to Daniel's, was the same as always. The same bedspread, the same curtains. The familiar Van Gogh print hung above the bed, showing two labourers resting in the shade of a golden haystack beneath a glorious blue sky.

Mum and Dad kept a framed family photo from a year ago on top of the chest of drawers. It was of all four of us, a favourite of theirs.

But it didn't look right.

I picked up the photo. There I was, a goofy grinning eleven-year-old. Dad was behind me, his hair under control for once. Mum had her arm round my shoulders. I knew that picture as well as I knew my own face.

Only I didn't, because Daniel wasn't in it.

I thought I was going to throw up. I stood with my eyes closed until my stomach stopped hurtling about. Then I set the photo carefully back on the chest of drawers.

There could only be one explanation. Somehow I'd entered a time layer where my brother didn't exist.

❧ ❧ ❧ ❧ ❧

I went downstairs, back to the farm office, back to the diary with the pages open at the twenty-fifth of August.

This time I checked the year.

It wasn't the August before the bulls came. It was the August after they did. I was in the next year. A whole year ahead of where I'd thought I was. I was already past the winter with the bulls.

I was a year older. I was thirteen, not twelve.

This time layer was in my future, not my past. And this future didn't include my brother.

Discovering the year kick-started something, and new memories of the preceding months, the months I hadn't really lived, flowed into my brain like water running across a beach.

I was remembering the life of the person I was going to be if I stayed in this time layer—not the person I was now.

I knew now why Daniel's bedroom was a spare room.

If I chose to stay here, in this time layer, I'd be a me who never had a brother.

But I wanted to have a brother.

The Cloak Pin

I was desperate to escape from the house and return to the Bull Stones. I had to get back to Tirvold's time layer and try to save Daniel some other way.

But first I wanted to go to the Long Mound and see what the archaeologists were doing. See what I could learn.

It was hard to hang on to the idea that I had a brother. The other memories, the future time layer memories, strengthened and took hold in my mind. The cold, sick feeling stayed in my stomach, but I had moments when I couldn't remember what was causing it.

In the kitchen, I struggled with the idea that I was supposed to do something, not remembering what it was. My mind was emptying. Grabbing at the thoughts slithering out of it was like trying to catch a bunch of wriggling fish by their tails—especially as the thoughts and memories from the future time layer were flooding in to replace them.

I shook my head hard, trying to restore some order.

Molly reappeared and mewed at me.

A new, future memory invaded my mind. Mum had left a casserole in the fridge for me to put in the oven. I glanced at the clock. It was getting close to when I had to think about putting the dinner on.

Molly wound around my calves again. I bent down to stroke her and something metal plopped out of my tee shirt pocket, ringing on the stone tiled floor.

It looked like an old key. I wondered why I'd put a key in my pocket, and picked it up.

The moment I had the metal object in my hand the time layers collided.

Everything clattered back into place. It wasn't a key. It was my cloak pin. As I held it, my real memories tried to force their way back. The Bull Stones, Tirvold, the Bullmaster.

Daniel.

I was on the verge of losing Daniel for ever. If I gave up now, I wouldn't have any memory of my brother. I stamped my feet, furious as the idea of abandoning him sneaked its way into me again like ivy smothering a wall.

Molly scampered away, stopping by the hallway door to glance back at me before running out. I gripped the cloak pin, bringing Daniel's face into my mind, confusing it with Tirvold's.

I pounded up the stairs two at a time, running to my room to snatch up my backpack and my jacket, then flying downstairs again and out to the orchard. I was terrified Mum or Dad would appear and I'd be trapped.

Free was still grazing, and she looked different. Her winter fur had vanished and she was fat, as though she'd been here all summer.

My hands shook so much I could hardly fasten the buckles as I tacked her up. I snatched up the blankets and my winter clothing and tied them behind the saddle.

I didn't dare put the cloak pin down even for a moment.

Holding it kept my real memories in place, though they felt as grey as shadows.

It would be hours yet before sundown, and I had a new fear. What if the moon, at this time of year, didn't fit the Moonstone. Suppose it had already risen too high by the time it was dark? Would that matter?

With hours to wait, I made for the archaeological site, riding with the cloak pin in one hand. Near the hill I realised I'd left my mobile charging in my room, but that was too bad. I wasn't going back.

The late afternoon brought a warm breeze. Despite everything, the ride made me feel better. Free flowed beneath me, her hooves beating their own rhythm on the summer-hardened ground. The wind was soft in my face, and the sun touched everything with a peculiar golden light that made the landscape more than three-dimensional.

I passed the Bull Stones and eased up to give Free a breather. She was sweating despite her new short coat. On the next rise, the archaeologists and their helpers were at work, well into the excavation.

No wonder the dig was bigger than I remembered. In this future time layer, they'd been working on it a whole extra summer.

I gave Free a loose rein and she picked her own pace up the hill, taking it slowly. It was about five o'clock and the workers were packing up for the day. I homed in on one, a young woman with a pleasant face and dark hair smoothed back in a ponytail.

I dismounted and led Free. The memories that I thought of as real, the ones I wanted to keep, were still being jostled by the intruder memories. I squeezed my cloak pin tighter and imagined a wall going up in my mind, shutting them out.

'Hi,' I said.

The woman was placing small tools into a canvas backpack. She smiled at me.

'Can you tell me a bit about the village?' I asked.

'It's Bronze Age,' she said. 'A very interesting site. It looks like it was abandoned after a battle. There's not much left of the buildings, but all the ones we've uncovered so far were burned. And we've found weapons, even bones. It's one of the most important sites anyone has ever found.'

Goose bumps clawed at my skin. Was the Bullmaster going to win after all? I put a hand on Free's shoulder to steady myself.

'What have you found?' I asked.

'Me personally?' she said. 'Not the most exciting stuff, but this was pretty good.'

She took out a notebook and flipped through it until she found the page she wanted.

'I found this yesterday,' she said proudly. 'This is a sketch of it.'

She held out the notebook and my heart exploded in my chest like a flock of pigeons scared by a hawk.

The woman's drawing was of my cloak pin, a little more twisted than I knew it to be, but it was the pin I was hiding in my hand. The clover shape, the three strands of bronze.

'Are you all right?' the woman asked, her brown eyes concerned. 'Are your parents around?'

I'd probably gone white.

'I'm fine,' I said. 'Just a bit hot. I live at the farm.'

Free began eating grass again, and I wiped my face. I was

trembling.

'It doesn't have to happen like that,' I said.

'Excuse me?' the woman said.

She looked at me hard, obviously wondering if she needed to summon help. I tried to clear my head. Sweat was streamed off me even though I was still only in my tee shirt and leggings. I swallowed.

'Sorry,' I said. 'I was thinking out loud. Do you know anything about the Long Mound?' The woman gave me a frowning look, but after a moment she answered.

'It's older than this village,' she said. 'We excavated it last summer and found some amazing things. The remains of three warriors in full battle dress, and lots of very exciting artefacts.'

She talked like a museum brochure.

'Did you — was there — anything like a helmet with bull's horns?' I asked.

The woman gave me another puzzled look. 'No.'

'Just wondered, with the Stone Circle being called the Bull Stones,' I said, feeling a need to explain the strangeness of my question.

'The Stone Circle's called the Bull Stones?' she said, frowning again. 'I never heard that.'

I felt as if the ground was falling away from under my feet.

'From that old legend, about the bulls appearing there one day in the seventeenth century,' I said. 'There was a feast...'

My voice trailed away. The story sounded like something I'd made up even to me, never mind to her, and she was still frowning, less and less certain about either my sanity or my honesty.

'Well, I've lived around here for ten years, and I've never

heard that,' she said. 'Everyone's leaving. I must go or I'll miss my bus.'

She shouldered her backpack and loped down the hill. I called out my last question. It should have been my first—but I was having trouble remembering why I wanted to know the answer.

'Is there a way into the Long Mound?'

She stopped, pushing stray hair behind her ear, looking back up the slope at me and giving me that assessing look again.

'Apart from the burial entrance, you mean?'

I nodded.

'No, that's it,' the woman said. 'Those huge slabs of stone at the end had an extraordinary design. There was a lever between them, a hidden iron handle. When you pulled it, the slabs slid on a system of rollers.'

She set off down the grassy slope again, answering me over her shoulder.

'But it's been blocked now that it's been excavated—there's no way in. They were afraid people would get trapped in there.'

She stopped again, facing me from a few metres away.

'Stay away from it,' she said. 'We did find the skeleton of a teenager, a boy. Not a warrior. No ceremonial burial, and for a short time we thought it might have been some relatively modern person, getting lost. The teeth were in surprisingly good condition.'

My heart thumped into my throat. Daniel had never had a filling in his life.

If I stayed in this time layer I'd be killing Daniel, not just preventing him from ever existing.

The woman tightened her backpack straps.

'But it does look as though he'd probably been there for about three thousand years,' she said. 'So perhaps he was someone who found his way in after the Mound fell into disuse, and became trapped.'

She set off again, wanting to catch up with her colleagues.

'It's that sort of puzzle that makes digging around in dirt so fascinating,' she yelled over her shoulder.

Left alone, I gazed at the Horse People's village, now little more than some trenches and excavated sections of earth. Inside, there was nothing above ground level and to me it didn't look like much at all.

I tried to imagine a fire, the village being abandoned.

Perhaps I was going back to be killed, dropping my cloak pin in the chaos for this archaeologist woman to find three thousand years later, along with the bones of my brother.

But it didn't matter. I had to return to the Bronze Age.

And now I knew how to open the Endstones.

In the late-falling dusk, I sat against one of the tilting blocks of the Bull Stones waiting for the moon to rise to the right place. The Stone vibrated and hummed gently against my back as though it was breathing. Gradually it soothed me and I felt stronger.

The lemon sunset crept away, leaving a Prussian blue sky releasing stars in every direction.

I held Free's reins in one hand, my cloak pin clamped in the other. The temperature of the cloak pin was the same as mine, and I only knew it was in my palm when I tightened my grip on it and felt the curve of it against my skin.

I rubbed my other hand against the Stone, a silent plea for it to help me, and the moon lined itself up.

It was the same, the travelling. I led Free quickly through the Stones and endured the wind noise and the ringing and the blurring. Did my horse feel it too?

The same winter night met me. I needed warm clothes immediately and put on my jacket.

When I ran my hands down Free's neck, she was furry again. The deep magic of the Stones had restored her winter coat. I swung up onto her back and rode to the Horse People's village.

Snow was falling heavily, the kind that looks great on a Christmas card. But I hardly noticed it through the churning in my head.

The village was quiet, with most people already in their huts for the night. A few stragglers still braved the snow in the village square, feeding the fire and singing their own winter songs. I steered clear of them and put Free back in the pen. Still no Molasses, just Deer.

I made my way to my hut. My friends the goats seemed pleased to see me, gazing into my face, bleating and tapping my feet with their little hooves. I found all my Bronze Age clothes where I'd left them and put them back on for warmth over my jacket.

I rolled myself into a horse blanket and lay down with the goats and dogs that shared the hut and their fleas with me. Not long afterwards, the other teenagers who slept there arrived too, barely glancing at me, and were quickly asleep.

I lay with my eyes open for a long time, one hand on the warm rough back of a goat sleeping against my side.

Far off in the frosty dark, the wolves sang their winter song.

Friends and Enemies

In the first light of the morning, I headed out to look for Rugal. I thought he'd be at the horse pen but he wasn't, and I didn't know where else to look.

Free neighed when she saw me. I bundled up an armful of the hay the Horse People stored in the nearby hut and gave it to her for breakfast. There was no sign of Molasses, so Tirvold was probably still missing. But Rugal's stallion was there, in his own pen.

I hurried to the main square to look for Rugal.

I encountered several people on the way. They turned their faces away from me, tugging their cloaks around them and speeding up as they passed.

Rugal was right. Nobody wanted to get involved with my problems.

At least now I dressed exactly like them, I no longer stood out. With my distinctive clothes hidden beneath my Bronze Age cloak and woven tunic, there was nothing visibly different about me. They probably thought I was from another village nearby. The village had other refugees from the Bullmaster's attacks.

If they thought about me at all. Their own survival was an all-consuming challenge at this time of year.

When I was almost at the square, I realised there was a person close behind me. He caught up, his face hidden by his cloak, which he'd drawn up like a hood.

'Do not trust Rugal,' he said softly.

I stopped so fast the man almost blundered into me. For a moment I thought he might be Tirvold, but even though the voice was low, I could tell it was different.

'Why not?' I asked.

'Rugal and Clynwas are poor,' the man said. 'The queen is rich, and her riches come from trading the horses that Rugal and Clynwas train. So now there is the greed feud.'

'Who are you?' I asked.

Abruptly, the man quickened his walk and took a side turn between some huts. I tried to follow, but he disappeared.

I remembered the scene by the fire on the first night, the near-fight when Clynwas threw Rugal the deer haunch. I was sure Rugal had enemies, and perhaps this was just one of the enemies, someone with a grudge.

After all, it was Tirvold who had arranged for the Bullmaster to capture Daniel. Not Rugal.

What if Tirvold was in contact with the Bullmaster? Was Tirvold on the other side, a traitor to his village?

Thinking about Daniel being captured by the Bullmaster pitched my anger off the back burner. I clenched my teeth hard enough to crack them as I hurried on.

There was no sign of Rugal in the main square, so I tried the horse pen again. This time he was there, his dog with him.

'I was waiting for you,' he said. 'I saw your horse was back. Did you go to your own time?'

'I tried,' I said, 'but it didn't work.'

At least I'd learnt there was a way to open the Endstones. Though what was the point of me doing that if the Bullmaster was in the Long Mound? And that was if I could even get to the Mound, with the bulls guarding it and happy to gore me to death if I tried.

Rugal wanted to know what I meant, when I said it didn't work. But whether it was the warning from the stranger or some instinct of my own, I brushed it off. And I said nothing about the Endstones and how they could be opened.

'I have to get Daniel out of the Long Mound,' I said.

'We must find Tirvold,' Rugal said. 'If we find him and bring the Bullmaster to understand that Tirvold is still free, he might let Daniel go.'

This sounded like the best plan I'd heard yet. Swap Tirvold for Daniel. And yet... I didn't like the idea of the Bullmaster killing anyone. Wouldn't he kill Tirvold?

'Why does Tirvold have to give himself up?' I said.

'Tirvold must fight his own fight,' Rugal said firmly. 'That is his destiny, and he must accept it. If it is right for him to win, he will win.'

I took my saddle and bridle from the hut and got Free ready. Rugal already had the bridle on Sostis and brought him out of his pen. He called his dog, then pulled back the poles that formed the gate of the main horse pen so I could lead Free out.

'How do we find Tirvold?' I said.

'There is a place near here where Eothal may be hiding,' Rugal said. 'Tirvold wants his sister to be queen. He is making a sacrifice of your brother, to buy time for his sister while she recovers. I know where she hides. If she is still there, he will be close.'

I mounted Free.

'What are we waiting for?' I said, and Rugal vaulted onto the back of his red stallion.

At least one person in the Bronze Age time layer was willing to help me.

We rode out of the village.

The Vision

The sky and the snow were a matching goose-grey, unruffled by wind, with the black bare trees separating them. The snow was softening, as though a thaw might be coming.

We neared the Mound and I concentrated on it, trying to open it with my mind, trying to coax Daniel out by imagining him running across the snow towards me.

My dream jumped at me, the dream about me or Daniel gliding across snow until a man raised his arm—his stone arm.

I shuddered. I recognised the gesture from the dream. It was the same one I saw the Bullmaster use to direct the bulls before he captured Daniel. That was why his gesture had looked familiar. I'd seen it first in my dream. How had I done that?

I shook off the thought. I didn't want to remember the dream.

I wanted to find a way to get rid of the bulls.

As we passed the Long Mound I tried to approach, but the bulls appeared from behind it and lined up, hostile and powerful. Free locked herself to the ground and resisted my attempts to urge her on.

Rugal was against it too.

'It is too dangerous,' he said. 'Your horse knows.'

'We did it the other day,' I objected. 'Yesterday, or whenever it was.'

Travelling between time layers was messing with my ability to keep up with the date.

'We were lucky,' Rugal said. 'It is rare that anyone can approach the Mound. If you try it now, the bulls will kill you.'

I wasn't all that interested in being killed by bulls.

I turned away, trying not to think about Daniel inside the Mound, twisting my fingers in Free's mane, silently promising my brother I'd save him. Somehow.

We rode on, the horses making a shushing sound in the soft snow, the dog trotting after us. The air was warmer than yesterday.

'It may be that Tirvold will recognise his destiny if you confront him,' Rugal said. 'He might even offer himself to the Bullmaster in Daniel's place.'

I was doubtful about that.

Tirvold hadn't worried too much about passing Daniel over to the Bullmaster to save his own skin in the first place. But perhaps there'd be a way of setting Tirvold up, doing the same thing to him, so I could get my brother back.

A tiny voice in my mind mentioned that if I really was Tirvold's descendant, I'd be trading one family member for another.

The argument banged about in my head. One was just some guy in the Bronze Age. The other was my brother.

But if Tirvold died and never had any descendants, what exactly would happen to me? Suppose I just vanished away, never existing in my time layer, never existing in their time layer, because Tirvold died?

'Let's race,' I said, to take my mind off it.

We raced, leaving the Mound and the bulls far behind, and I

won. Rugal had a stallion and should have been faster, but my mare was an Arabian with three thousand more years of strength and stamina bred into her, and she hadn't endured two months of Bronze Age winter.

'With a mare like that, I would begin a line of great horses,' Rugal said admiringly.

We'd stopped under a stand of trees where the ground was almost clear of snow to eat. Lunch was flat, dry bread and cold boar meat. The dog drooled anxiously a couple of metres from us. He was grateful even for gristle scraps, and I sneaked him a large piece of meat while Rugal's back was turned.

It was a day that made me feel tiny in the snow. The sky was a strange light grey and the air luminescent. It was like being in the hollow centre of a huge pearl.

We rode on all afternoon. At first we chatted, but after a while we rode in complete silence. The light was turning the colour of tin, the beginning of dusk falling, when we came to a wedge of trees stacked thickly along the curve of the hill.

Rugal rode along the border of the woods, peering between the knitted trunks. Then he turned his horse down a track that was hardly wide enough to call a track, his dog close behind. I followed, bending low over Free's neck as we scraped beneath branches.

We arrived in a small clearing with a shelter in it, a low round hut built with snow and partly covered with dead branches. Rugal said nothing and raised his hand to signal to me to be quiet as well. He dropped lightly off his horse and moved softly to the doorway.

I dismounted and followed him, my heart thumping in my

throat, slow and scared.

The inside of the snow hut was peaceful. I could almost feel a little warmth in the air.

'This is the place,' Rugal said.

There was an edge to his voice. Hearing it, I looked across the hut and caught a gleam of anger in his eyes. It vanished so fast that I might not have understood what I was seeing if his voice hadn't given him away.

'They escaped,' he said. 'I should have come sooner.'

He pushed past me and called his dog.

I followed him outside. He was casting about in the snow with the dog, searching for tracks. I waited, my stomach a cold pit. The woods bent over us, silent and gloomy.

There was some undercurrent that I didn't understand.

'They went during the snowfall last night,' Rugal said at last. 'There is almost nothing to follow.'

He sent the dog into the hut and out, trying for scent. He turned to me, and once again he seemed like the Rugal I'd come to trust. His eyes no longer looked like glass chips. They shone warm and green in his copper-freckled face. He smiled.

'Let us go after them, Lizzie Brave,' he said. 'We will find Tirvold and save your brother.'

We mounted our horses. It was a relief to ride out into the open again.

Beyond the trees, we halted again. I loitered on Free while Rugal, staying on Sostis, looked for tracks or scent with the dog, making wider and wider ripples like pebbles in a snow-pond.

A pattern of rooks stippled the sky above the trees, the wind carrying their hoarse voices to me.

Free took a few steps. She liked Sostis and wanted to stay within a comfortable distance. I let her wander on.

We trailed along slowly, nearing the black shackles of the next belt of trees. Rugal was up ahead, still working with his dog.

Free pricked her ears, staring into the monochrome, silent wood to my left.

I stared too—at first I thought it was a trick of the shadows.

But there was a figure.

Motionless, upright, and dressed like Tirvold. His arms were as limp as a sleepwalker's.

The rooks cawed in the distance.

I saw a white face, a body drained by sadness and cold. My brother.

'Daniel!' I said.

My heels thumped into Free's ribs, but she didn't move.

Daniel gazed at me, or through me. He didn't seem to see me.

'I am lost and cannot be found,' he said.

I heard it as a whisper, although the distance between us was so great I'd barely have heard a shout from him.

'I am lost and cannot be found,' he whispered again.

It was so close, right in my ears, that I turned my head quickly to see if somehow he was right behind me. But he wasn't. Icy tears spilled down my cheeks.

Free wouldn't move. She might have been carved from stone, staring at Daniel—if it was Daniel—with her ears pricked.

'Daniel, come toward me,' I whispered.

He turned away, gliding, and dissolved into the emptiness between the trees.

My dream. I was seeing him in my dream, the man with the

stone arm waiting for him.

With a jolt, I heard and saw everything around me again.

Heard the dog baying, heard Rugal shouting he'd found the tracks he wanted. Free stirred beneath me, heading for Rugal and his horse.

I flung myself off her back and ran headlong across the wasteland into the trees, but Daniel had vanished.

Under the first bone branches, I tripped and fell in the empty, unforgiving snow.

Closing In

When it was very dark, we stopped riding and camped on the edge of a hill by a sluggish river. We were far out on our own in a wild forest.

Rugal said he'd maintain a watch during the night against wolves. We tied the horses near us, and they dug under the snow for grass while we gathered enough wood to build a monster fire. I sat beside it in Free's blanket, Rugal's dog at my feet. The flames made me warm for the first time that day.

We faced out across the hills, forest-black and cloud-dulled. No stars tonight, and no moon.

And somewhere, in the darkest dark of all, my brother.

I took a branch and poked the fire.

'Who is the Bullmaster?' I asked.

Rugal was still, one hand loosely holding his bow.

'He is the Bullmaster,' he said, without showing much interest. 'There has always been a feud between the Bullmaster and the family of Tirvold.'

Tirvold said there was feud between his family and Rugal's, and the Bullmaster wanted gold and the village. Did this mean Rugal's family sided with the Bullmaster? That couldn't be right.

My head ached from exhaustion and hunger, throbbing each

time I moved. I lay down, my back to the heat. The ins and outs of feuds in a time long before my own were too much for me to unravel.

I curled up with the blanket tight around me, trying to come up with a plan to rescue Daniel. None of my ideas seemed any good to me.

Perhaps there was some way to get the Bullmaster to chase Tirvold the way he'd chased us on the way back from the boar hunt. With the Bullmaster distracted, I might have time to get into the Long Mound and find Daniel.

I was snatching at straws, but it seemed more possible to me than trying to trade Tirvold for my brother. I couldn't picture Tirvold buying into that, and we couldn't force him to do it.

Maybe it was too late. Maybe Daniel had told the Bullmaster how to use the Stones and was already dead. Lost and not to be found. A wight.

'Daniel,' I whispered into the flames. 'Don't tell him.'

'What?' Rugal said. He had called his dog to him and was sitting with his back to me on the other side of the fire. Watching for wolves.

I closed my eyes and pretended to sleep.

I could hardly bring myself to picture Daniel alone in the death-dark of the Long Mound. In a cold stone tomb perhaps, with warriors turning to dust around him. He must know I would do everything possible to save him from such a fate.

But I had no idea how to do it and I was beginning to fear I might never be able to rescue him.

I felt as lost as Daniel. At least Rugal was on my side.

In the coldest hours of the night, in the hunter dark, I heard the distant crying of the wolves. Longing filled their voices, and I lay rolled in the blanket beneath an impenetrable sky, wondering what it was they longed for. They sounded as though they knew it was gone forever.

❧❧ ❧❧ ❧❧ ❧❧ ❧❧ ❧❧

Rugal killed a long-limbed snowy white hare in the morning with a single arrow through the chest. He skinned and cleaned it, feeding the parts we wouldn't eat to his dog, rebuilt the fire, and spitted the meat over it. We hadn't eaten the night before and hunger wrenched me to the core.

The hare sizzled. The sweet blue smoke sought the sky, which was as pale and fragile as an eggshell. The savoury smell of the meat made my mouth water.

'Tirvold will destroy our village,' Rugal said.

He was sitting on his haunches before the flames, poking the meat with a blade of stone. I squatted like him, exhausted and cold, half my mind on Free, who was making a poor breakfast beside Sostis off the flat frozen grasses beneath the snow.

'What do you mean?' I asked.

'He wants control,' Rugal said. 'It is more important to him than saving the village from the Bullmaster. The woman he wants to be queen is his sister. If she were not his sister, he would not be fighting for her.'

'But if she does become queen, won't she try to save the village from the Bullmaster?'

I could hear my hesitation in my voice. It was all so confusing—who was on the good side?

'It is possible,' Rugal said. 'But she cannot win. The Bullmaster is too powerful. There is too much on his side. Tirvold should give up.'

Rugal turned over the split, spitted hare. My mouth was watering so much I could hardly think.

'The Bullmaster has conquered other villages,' he said. 'They will fight with him. The Horse People are too few.'

I thought of the burnt village the archaeologists had found and shifted on my heels, wrapping my cloak tighter. Even with the thaw, which had set in properly, it was still cold, and now the air was thick with a damp rawness too.

'Why hasn't the Bullmaster won already?' I said.

'Tirvold's father and the former queen Emoral fought him and won the first battle,' Rugal said. 'The Bullmaster lacks the power of the Stone Circles, which is the power to move beyond our time. Once he controls the magic, his own power will be complete, and nothing can stop him.'

Two of us knew how to wield that power. Tirvold the Keeper of the Stones, and me.

Rugal tested the meat, poking a chunk with his knifepoint.

'The Bullmaster will destroy the village if he can't find Tirvold,' he said. 'Tirvold should save the village by offering himself.'

Tirvold, my not so noble ancestor. His genes were my genes. Was I like him?

'What's so bad about the Bullmaster anyway?' I asked.

Rugal frowned. 'He makes all men slaves,' he said. 'Everything we own would belong to him. Our gold.'

He slid a fingertip along his neck ring. 'But it is said a chosen few will be spared,' he said. 'Those who work for him.'

In the silence, I heard the thin wild mew of a hawk, and squinted up against the pallid sun to look for it.

'The meat is ready,' Rugal said.

We ate half the hare each, the taste of it as good as anything I'd ever had. I gulped it down like Rugal's dog, and felt my spirits rise with each hot half-chewed chunk. We sucked everything we could off the bones and then the dog crunched those up too.

We got the horses ready and set off, and soon Rugal again picked up the tracks that he said belonged to Tirvold and Eothal. He dismounted and knelt in the shallow skeins of disappearing snow.

'Here is the hoof-print of Daniel's horse,' he said. 'It is bigger than any in our village, and it has that metal part.'

'Horseshoes,' I said. Molasses. He was safe. 'To protect his feet. Can you tell if he's still lame?'

Rugal had leashed his dog, to stop it fouling the tracks. He took a few cautious steps, intent on the ground.

'I think he is better,' he said. 'They are travelling fast.'

He went down on one knee again, and touched something on the muddy ground between the snow patches that to me, from Free's back, was nothing more than an indistinct smudge.

'Eothal is riding her own horse,' he said. 'A bay mare. I trained the mare, and this is her track. They are taking a westward course, and it may be they passed by as recently as yesterday.'

'Yesterday!' I cried. 'Do you think we'll catch up with them today?'

'No,' Rugal said. 'They are still fast and far ahead of us.' He smiled at me, but his eyes flashed with quickly-hidden anger, as cold as green ice. And for the first time, he made me afraid.

The Village of Death

Late in the day, emerging from a stretch of scrubby woodland, we gazed down a long snowy slope at a settlement.

'I have friends in this village,' Rugal said. 'We can stay there tonight.'

It was larger than the Horse People's village. Perhaps a hundred small huts crouched behind the same type of stockade fence that the Horse People had built around their hilltop.

But at this place, men stood guard all around the perimeter. They saw us coming, and as we rode closer, more faces appeared at the fence, more people with spears in hand.

'Are they Horse People too?' I asked cautiously.

Rugal didn't answer.

I scanned their faces, looking for welcome or even curiosity. Rugal had said they were friends, but there was nothing. Old or young, they were pale and expressionless. They showed no reaction to our arrival, not even looking at me.

'You must stop here,' Rugal said.

I halted Free. She fretted in the thawing snow and mud, not wanting to be separated from Sostis. Rugal rode the last ten metres to the gate. Two of the men opened it. Like the Horse People's village, rails on the inside held it shut. Then the gatekeepers waited, heads bent, staring at the ground.

Bowing? It hardly seemed likely, although Rugal was related to royalty.

But their manner was disturbing and strange, almost robotic. I found myself checking Free more roughly than I needed to. I couldn't concentrate on what was going on with her fidgeting and twisting beneath me.

The village men moved in slow motion, awkward and dull. Rugal talked to two of them. I couldn't hear what he said, or their mumbled replies. They stood with their heads bowed, arms by their sides.

When I glanced at the spear-holders, they'd all gone back to their watch positions, and were paying no attention to Rugal. Motionless, cold, lost in their task.

Rugal turned and called me in. I trotted Free over and we passed through the gate into the silent village.

A chill descended on me. The sun faded behind opaque cloud cover that I hadn't noticed until then. The air pressed against my skin, heavy and cold.

At the edge of my senses, I caught a distant smell of mould, of something horrible. Musty, dead, closed up. My insides froze, numbing me beyond thought.

The sensation passed, and I realised Rugal had touched my arm. He didn't seem to have noticed any smell or strangeness.

'Sorry,' I mumbled. 'I felt sort of shaky.'

'You are tired,' Rugal said gently. 'We will eat and then rest.'

I'd thought the Horse People lived a hard life. But their village looked like a five-star resort next to this one. Many of the huts along the dead and rat-infested pathways of this village were empty. Some were derelict, the roofs fallen in, snowdrifts in the living spaces.

Again the foul suggestion of a smell brushed against me. It was how earth might stink after something rotten was pulled from it, a death-stench. My stomach twisted, anticipating the worst.

But the next breath I took was clean winter air. It didn't smell great because of the village's unwashed and rubbishy odour, but it wasn't the death-stench.

We passed two men with grey clothes and white, thin faces. I tried to smile, but their eyes were empty and they weren't looking at me. They stood close together, limp and hopeless, by one of the more usable huts.

Rugal ignored them. It was obvious he knew his way around, and he led me to an empty stock pen. We released our horses in it, and they sniffed at a heap of damp, old hay in the middle. Apparently it was too decayed to be edible and they left it, standing with hanging heads.

I leant on the fence, wishing I could provide something for Free to eat. Wishing I didn't feel so washed out.

'Come,' Rugal said.

He pointed in the direction of a hut with smoke rising from it, and strode off with his dog at his heels. I followed too, wanting to sleep more than anything in the world.

'Where is everybody?' I asked.

Rugal looked away.

'There was a sickness,' he said. 'Many people died.'

'It looks like most of the village,' I said.

My head was throbbing again. I had a dull longing to lie down that was almost irresistible.

Rugal shrugged. 'There is always death.'

Here, it felt like there was more than death.

We entered the hut and met one of the men Rugal had talked to at the gate. I sat by the fire and looked around. There was nothing in the hut. No bed, no furs, no pots – just the fire, and that was newly lit.

The man, so thin that his skin was like wax paper over his bones, handed me a sliver of unidentifiable dried meat and a piece of hard bread. I tried to thank him but his opaque, dark eyes would not meet mine.

It came to me this was his own meal and he'd been ordered to give it to me.

I shook my head and handed it back to him. He hesitated, then accepted it and bowed his head. Holding the food in one hand, he rose. As he reached the door, I saw him tear at the meat with his teeth the way Rugal's dog had torn at the pieces of hare.

I had Free's blanket with me and rolled myself up in it. The dog tucked himself up against me. I was willing to share his fleas in exchange for his warmth.

'Why didn't we just camp out again?' I said. 'This is a horrible place. They're all afraid of something.'

Rugal gave me a hard look.

'I cannot stay awake a second night to watch for wolves,' he said.

But his irritation didn't affect me. I was more exhausted than I'd ever been in my life, and fleas or not, I was already plunging headlong into the subterranean worlds of sleep.

During the night, when the fire was almost out, I woke up

sweating. I'd been having the dream about Daniel again. As I lay there, taking deep breaths to calm myself, the death-stench found me, running its sickening fingers into my nose and mouth.

I thought I was going to throw up. I sat up dizzily. I heard a moaning sound and realised it was coming from me. I held my breath, afraid to take another, but when I finally had to, it was just the smoky air of the hut. The death-stench had gone.

I lay down again and as I fell back into sleep, I noticed I was alone.

ℯ℮ ℯ℮ ℯ℮ ℯ℮ ℯ℮ ℯ℮

At dawn, I drifted into wakefulness and found Rugal there, also waking. Perhaps he had been there throughout the night after all. It all seemed strange and unreal anyway. We left after a break-fast of hard bread. I was too hungry not to eat this time, even if I was depriving somebody else of food.

In the middle of the morning, Rugal halted his horse and pointed at a long swan's neck of woodland.

'There,' he said. 'We found them.'

I followed his pointing arm and saw Tirvold and a girl that presumably was his sister, Eothal the queen. And two horses. Free recognised Molasses and neighed. He threw up his head and neighed back.

I was so pinched with weariness I hardly knew whether to feel relieved, afraid, or hopeful. I didn't feel much at all.

We approached, and they waited for us.

They were both wary and unsmiling. Tirvold was riding Mo-lasses. Eothal was pale-faced on her bay mare, which was smaller and shaggier than I'd pictured. I'd forgotten that even for queens, in this time layer only Bronze Age horses existed.

Eothal wasn't sitting her horse well. She slumped, unbalanced and lopsided, and I remembered the bronze-horned bull had gored her in the thigh.

'So,' Tirvold said, 'you followed us and found us.'

Rugal didn't reply. Tirvold's face, so like Daniel's, was clenched with repressed anger. It was like having Daniel angry with me.

'You have to help me save my brother,' I blurted out.

Tirvold looked aside, then at Rugal, his fury intense and palpable. I appealed instead to his sister, the queen.

'The Bullmaster captured my brother,' I said. 'Tirvold tricked him. He tricked the Bullmaster. My brother's in the Long Mound and he'll die if I don't rescue him.'

Eothal's look was cold and imperious, and she remained silent. Her aquiline beauty pierced me.

'I can't do it by myself,' I said desperately.

'We do not know whether we can trust your brother,' Tirvold said. 'He might reveal how to use the power of the Stones.'

'What?' I said, fury bubbling through me like lava. 'You're the one that got him captured in the first place. He'd never get someone else in trouble like that. There's no way he's going to help the Bullmaster.'

'Your brother faces death,' Tirvold said. 'There is no knowing how people behave when they face death.'

His hands tightened on the reins and Molasses tossed his head. Eothal stirred, pushing herself straighter on her horse's back, easing her right leg. I saw that Tirvold had taken Daniel's saddle off Molasses and put it on Eothal's horse, to help her.

'Some are brave and some are not,' Eothal said. Her voice was low, but it was clear. 'Your brother has no ties to our people. Why should he not tell the Bullmaster what he knows if he thinks it will save his life?'

We did have family ties to Tirvold and Eothal, but neither of them knew that. And nor did Daniel, I realised.

'You're the Keeper of the Stones,' I said to Tirvold. 'You know how the deep magic works and so do I. But Daniel doesn't. He can't tell the Bullmaster anything.'

I became conscious of Rugal again, outside our circle. Watching me. Listening to us. Somewhere in the trees, a magpie squawked.

I was holding Free's reins too tightly and she was upset, my tension reaching her. I loosened my grip.

'Why did you set him up?' I said, trying to sound calm.

'Set him up?' Tirvold said.

I couldn't tell whether he was playing dumb or truly puzzled by the expression.

'Yes,' I said. 'Didn't you tell the Bullmaster? You made Daniel dress in clothes like yours. You made him ride your horse. And then the Bullmaster came and thought he was you.'

'It is not true,' Tirvold said, looking shocked that I'd think he'd planned it all. 'Daniel's horse went lame. How could I arrange that?'

In front of me was Molasses, kind Molasses who would do anything for anyone. I wanted to get down and hug him, check he was all right. Nothing was going how I'd hoped anyway.

In the silence, my anger drained away, almost taking me with it down a black bottomless hole. I rubbed my eyes with the heel of my hand. No way was I going to let them see any tears. I took a fierce breath.

Tirvold turned Molasses towards the trees.

'Since we are all together now, we should stay together,' he said. 'We are on our way to seek help for Eothal from a healer, a woman skilled in herbal cures. But first, we need to hunt for food.'

Nothing was resolved. Daniel was forgotten by everyone except me.

Why had I expected Tirvold to apologise and say he'd do whatever it took to get Daniel out of the Mound? I should have stayed at the village, close to my brother.

Instead I was caught up in their journey to find help for Eothal, unless Rugal would come back with me. I couldn't go back on my own, spending two nights in the open, not knowing the way.

Being eaten by wolves…

The Wounded Queen

If there was one benefit to the Bronze Age time layer it was the amount of wildlife, and it was only a few minutes before Rugal, whose archery skills were seriously good, killed a deer. We slung it behind him on his horse until we reached a place to camp for the night, with water in a half-frozen stream for both ourselves and the horses.

Rugal and Tirvold prepared the deer and cooked chunks over a fire they started laboriously in their usual way, chipping sparks from flints into dry tinder they carried with them.

Hobbled, the horses scraped for winter grass under the snow or gnawed tree bark. They were desperately hungry. I'd been plunged into remorse by the feel of Molasses's ribs beneath his winter coat. In only a few days, he was much thinner.

I realised I was thinner too. The Bronze Age was short of cakes and biscuits.

Tirvold had helped Eothal off her horse. She more or less fell and it was obvious, though they tried to hide it, that she could barely support herself. They sat together by the fire, tending the spitted meat and talking in voices too low for either Rugal or me to hear.

We'd hauled up enough wood to make ourselves a ring of

fires against wolves. At nightfall, we'd bring the horses in close, but for now we let them forage for what they could find to eat.

The waning afternoon gave us up to a river of bitter wind. In the remaining half-light, I went off alone, armed with a burning branch, to check on Free and Molasses.

On the way back I spotted tracks in the snow, and bent over them.

My heart slowed to a dull, horrible thudding.

Bull tracks.

Well, maybe there were cows around here.

They could only be bull tracks.

I looked up at the others, far off in the gloom, Rugal and Tir-vold trudging around lighting the fire ring.

I couldn't bear to look behind me. I trained every nerve on making it back to the camp instead. Every slow step a slushy squelch in the melting snow. Back to the others.

Squelch.

Fighting the urge to run.

Squelch.

A whisper.

'Your way is wrong.'

Clear in the cold air, it was right next to me in the dark. I whirled around, forgetting the bull tracks.

'Daniel?' I said.

But there was nothing around me except snow, trees, sky, and the night fallen over everything.

I couldn't see Daniel, but I could hear him. His voice was slow and distant, but at the same time it sounded as though he was beside me.

'Lizzie, your way is wrong,' Daniel said. 'Help me.'

Open snow, dark sky, trees meshed in between.

A quiet wrapped around me, until Rugal shouted.

'Lizzie Brave! Do you see something?'

I turned. Rugal was halfway between me and the camp, hesitating.

My head cleared.

'No,' I said. 'Just imagining things. Wolves, or whatever.'

Walking towards him, I had time in the dark to straighten my face into something believable.

What did Daniel mean, my way was wrong?

ᘓᘔ ᘓᘔ ᘓᘔ ᘓᘔ ᘓᘔ ᘓᘔ

We ate part of the deer, and stored the rest in snow so it would freeze and we could take it with us in the morning. Afterwards, with Rugal and Tirvold wordlessly collecting wood and heaping it on the fires, I sat down near Eothal.

If I could get Eothal on my side, perhaps she'd talk Tirvold into helping me free Daniel. Your way is wrong. Somehow I had to find the right way.

'How are you feeling?' I said. 'You didn't eat much.'

Not like the rest of us, I might have added. I had half a haunch of venison lying in my stomach, satisfyingly heavy. It wasn't often you had enough to eat in the Bronze Age.

Her shoulders half-inched up, dropped, in a shadow of a shrug.

'My leg is very painful,' she said. 'It was not ready for me to ride, but I must reach the healer soon.'

The hooting of tawny owls soothed the night, broken by the

occasional yapping of a fox. The air was cold enough to rub between your fingers like feathers. I unfolded my horse blanket
and offered to share it with Eothal. She shook her head.

'Thank you,' she said. 'No. I am warm enough.'

She glanced at Tirvold and Rugal, who were talking something over. Tirvold had his knife out and was carving one of his
wooden animals. His back was taut. Rugal looked away, one hand
drumming a rapid, silent beat on his wool-clad knee. It didn't
look like a friendly conversation.

I dragged my attention back to Eothal.

'Maybe I could look at your leg tomorrow, when it's light,' I
offered. 'I'm quite used to wounds, on animals anyway. We have
a farm and there's always an animal to patch up.'

'I need certain herbs,' she said. 'Medicine.'

'And the healer can help?' I asked.

'Perhaps,' Eothal said, 'but a Bullwound means death.'

Did she really mean that? She said it with such acceptance.

I bit my lower lip, still looking for the right moment to speak
about Daniel, but Eothal touched my hand and I met her eyes
again. Even in the golden glow from the fire her face was drawn
in shades of ash, pale where her skin strained over her bones,
dark in the hollows.

'Tirvold is not running away,' she said quietly. 'You must not
think he has abandoned your brother. You must trust him. Not
Rugal.'

'But Tirvold set a trap for Daniel,' I said.

Eothal frowned. I hauled the blanket tighter around me to
stop myself trembling.

'He left us so the Bullmaster would take Daniel,' I said.

'Rugal's the only one who's been willing to help me.'

In the silence of the snow I heard Eothal's shallow, urgent breathing.

'You think that is why Rugal is here?' she asked. 'To help you?'

I said nothing. Of course she was going to defend her brother.

'I need the aid of a healer,' Eothal said quietly. 'But the Bull-master does not want me healed. So Rugal is here, to keep watch.'

Behind me, on one of the fires, a wet piece of wood was re-leasing a sappy hiss as it heated up. Rugal and Tirvold were no longer talking. Far off, I heard the first howls of wolves.

Eothal said nothing for so long that I lay down, ready to sleep beneath the star-encrusted sky, lulled by the soft sound of the horses breathing behind me and the gentle hooting of the owls. I jumped when she spoke again.

'We are your friends, Tirvold and I,' she whispered.

It reminded me I was probably descended from Tirvold, or even Eothal, though I looked more like Rugal than her, with her dark hair and blue eyes. I'd have liked to have inherited her wide, slanted, royal cheekbones.

She lowered herself to the ground in stages, trying to stifle small groans of pain and refusing my help. I knew I wouldn't be riding a horse and camping out in snow if it hurt me that much just to lie down.

The moon rose and washed us in a waterfall of silver, and in its hollow light the wolves howled.

18

The Bullwound

At dawn, with the air cutting like metal, Tirvold and Rugal hung some of the partly frozen deer meat over the flames until it warmed enough for us to gnaw chunks for breakfast. They bound up the rest in a sheepskin.

I led our four horses to the creek to drink. There was no flat place to stand and they balanced awkwardly with their hindquarters up the bank. Free lifted her head, holding water in her mouth because she hadn't finished drinking, and gave me a nudge.

'I know,' I said, trying to reassure myself as much as my horse. 'You're hungry, and it's all weird, and you can't see the end of it. Nor can I, but I have to get Daniel back.'

I left the horses clipping the short winter grass that was emerging from the snow and trudged the few metres back to the fire. Eothal was sitting up, withdrawn in her cloak and furs, her face dull with suffering.

I sat down beside her and put my hand tentatively on her arm.

'Eothal, show me your leg. Perhaps I can do something.'

She nodded, her eyes clouded and dark with pain.

Gently I parted her cloak's folds, trying not to let in too much cold air, although there seemed to be no warmth to let out. Eothal was wearing the same woollen trousers we all wore but hers were torn, and it had to be from the goring of the bull because the cloth was stiff and dark with dried blood.

The swollen wound in her thigh appalled me. It was a mess, deep and burning with infection, far beyond anything I could deal with here. The pain of it must be unbearable, and she had been riding for three days.

Seeing it, I believed for the first time that she might die.

'It is bad, is it not?' she said.

'Yes, it's bad,' I said, too shocked to lie.

I wrapped the cloak around her again.

When I looked across at the others, Tirvold was watching us. He was immobile, and I was close enough to read his face. He too saw death ahead of her.

Now I understood the fear I'd seen in him.

Eothal refused food. I took a bronze cup from her belongings and filled it with water from the creek. She drank it so fast I was afraid it would come straight back up again. When I pushed her hair back from her forehead and rested my palm there, her skin was almost hot enough to brand me.

I thought of antibiotics and painkillers, thousands of years away in a time layer I couldn't get to without the Stones. I'd never grumble about a headache again.

We brought the horses in and got them ready.

'Eothal's very ill,' I said quietly to Tirvold. 'She has a high fever.'

'We will reach the village with the healer this morning,' he said. 'It is a small village but it has little, so it is still free from the Bullmaster.'

I rode by Eothal's side through the morning, talking to her, helping her stay on her horse, giving her water when we stopped to rest. Several times she swayed and flopped in the saddle and I wondered whether I should put her on Free and sit behind her to hold her on. The last thing Eothal needed was a fall.

We arrived at the village at midday. I wanted to get Rugal alone, to talk to him about persuading Tirvold to step in with the Bullmaster. Daniel's presence wouldn't leave me, standing untouchable, invisible, at the edge of the forest while his whisper tore through me.

And I was worried about being so far from the Stones. Daniel had said I was going the wrong way and I didn't know what else it could mean.

Tirvold dismounted and came to me quietly. He touched my hand, a gesture of hope. When he spoke, the strain so great in his voice that he was barely audible.

'You have seen the Bullwound,' he said. 'Please go with Eothal. A man cannot enter the house of the healer unless he is sick himself. It is the province of women.' I nodded.

'Where will you be?' I said.

'Rugal and I will go and offer our greetings to the village elder,' Tirvold said. 'We must make a gift of the deer meat.'

A young girl swathed in woollen garments led Eothal and me, still on horseback, to the healer. At the hut I dismounted and eased Eothal, semi-conscious, to the ground. The girl left with our horses. I hoped she'd feed them.

With one of Eothal's arms over my shoulders so I could grip her limp hand and my other arm around her waist, I helped her

into the hut. Her legs buckled at every step, but it didn't matter. She was a featherweight, burned dry and light as charcoal by fever, and I'm as strong as anyone raised on a farm.

The healer was younger than I expected, about Mum's age and with something of her composure. The resemblance, slight as it was, almost overwhelmed me.

The healer indicated a raised bench padded with animal furs. 'Let her lie there,' she said.

Her voice was low and thoughtful. She'd tied her brown hair the way Eothal wore hers, plaited with coloured cloth. As my eyes got used to the fire-glow, I saw bunches of herbs and other dried plants hanging in dense masses from the ceiling. The sharp dry scent of them mingled with the smell of wood smoke.

The healer knelt by Eothal, who lay with her eyes shut, her breathing slight and irregular. She was drenched in sweat and occasionally mumbling, not focusing on what was going on around her.

'My name is Marantis,' the healer said to me. 'I will help her if I can. What is her illness?'

I knelt beside her, opening Eothal's cloak.

'It's her leg,' I said. 'She was gored by a bull.'

Marantis lowered her gaze. 'Ah.'

She rose and fetched a burning branch from the fire to give us more light. We examined Eothal's injury in silence. Even in the last day or so, the infection had worsened. Eothal muttered indistinct words, seeming unaware of our presence as we studied her.

'A Bullwound is severe,' Marantis murmured. 'And it is the hardest to treat, because there is magic in it.'

Nothing that the magic of antibiotics wouldn't handle, I thought. If only I'd brought some from our farm back through the Stones with me. But I hadn't known, had I?

Marantis was sorting through the herbs hanging from the ceiling, stroking the bunches of dry, fragrant leaves as though they were her friends.

'I will try,' she said. 'But those who suffer the Bullwound must die.'

My throat closed, and I looked at Eothal to see if she had heard. Her eyes were open and met mine. I reached out and took her hand from where it was wilting on the wolf skin, and her hot, dry fingers locked round mine with the iron grip of fear.

The Return

For two days Marantis treated Eothal, while I grew more and more anxious about Daniel. Tirvold sought me out several times for updates on his sister's condition.

The community was smaller than the Horse People's village. They too held communal evening fires and feasting, and shared their lives with animal life from cows to rats.

At least our horses, especially poor hungry Molasses, had hay, some kind of dry grass that the people here cut and stored for winter as the Horse People did.

At the horse pen, Rugal pointed out a couple of bays and a dun horse similar to Tirvold's horse Deer.

'Those three I trained, and these people bought them last summer, from the queen,' he said. 'There is no one who can train a horse the way I can.'

I believed it.

'If I owned the horses I train so I could sell them myself, I would be rich,' he said.

I was too twitchy about my brother, spending what felt like a lifetime trapped in a burial mound, to get into Rugal's career gripes.

'It's been days and days,' I said, ripping wood splinters off the fence. 'What about food? Or water?'

'There is plenty,' Rugal said, a little taken aback. 'The hay is good too.'

'Not for the horses,' I said, 'for Daniel.'

'The Bullmaster has magic to keep him alive,' Rugal said.

He reached out and put his palm on top of my restless hand to still it.

'I will help you save your brother,' he said. 'So you do not need to tear the fence apart to persuade me.'

℮℮ ℮℮ ℮℮ ℮℮ ℮℮ ℮℮

Marantis took me on as a helper. She showed me how to clean and dress Eothal's leg with the herbs, ground to a powder between flat stones and made into a thick paste with honey, and prepare frequent doses of some kind of herbal tea. Eothal drank little, but often.

Marantis never questioned me about my origins. I wondered about that, and then decided she must think I was one of the Horse People. There would be no reason for her to think anything else.

Eothal's fever broke and her temperature returned to normal. By the end of the second day, she was able to stand and even take a few shaky steps with some support. Her wound appeared cleaner and less inflamed. Eothal assured us the pain was less.

On the morning of the third day, Tirvold paid Marantis with a knob of gold, and she dressed Eothal's wound for the last time with her medicines and bound it with cloth. She gave Eothal a supply of dried herbs and honey, and we took our horses and some food supplies and rode away.

We took the quickest route we could, though we had to ride slowly to spare Eothal. But we only camped out for one night. On the second morning, passing a knoll I thought I recognised, I pointed it out to Eothal.

'Is there a village over there?' I asked.

I hadn't told them I'd stayed overnight in one with Rugal.

Eothal nodded, not looking in that direction and urging her horse into a canter.

'We are too close to it,' she said. 'It is a village that has fallen to the Bullmaster.'

I was silenced, battling again with the feeling that I didn't know what was going on. If it was the village I'd stayed in with Rugal, why would he take me to a place the Bullmaster held? Surely it would be dangerous for him—never mind me?

I told myself the snowy landscape had confused me, and it wasn't the same village at all. And then I tried to forget it.

꽃 꽃 꽃 꽃 꽃 꽃

We rode unnoticed into the Horse People's village at dusk on the second day. Eothal's fever had returned, and the healer's words about the Bullwound always leading to death ran through my brain, as endless as wire.

20

Thief

When I went through the Stones again, it was to get antibiotics from my time layer for Eothal.

I couldn't help hoping I'd arrive at a slightly different point, find Daniel at home, and be able to change events by stopping the mad calendar escapade before it happened. I took Molasses with me as well as Free, so at least he had a chance of a decent meal.

With the hope there was guilt. If Daniel was there, I wouldn't go back to the Bronze Age to try to save Eothal's life.

I carried the cloak pin with me to make sure that this time, I didn't forget what I needed to remember.

It was a spring afternoon when I arrived, overcast and threatening to rain, and I rode fast down the hill towards the farm, leading Molasses beside Free. I knew immediately that I wasn't in exactly the right time layer, because there was no sign of the archaeology dig on the hill.

The house was different too.

The windowsills were painted pale blue instead of the white I'd always known, and the tractor in the farmyard was an older model, but looked new. Two Border collies I didn't recognise sprinted around the corner of the house, hackles up, barking. I tossed them chunks of dried deer meat from my backpack and their attitude became much friendlier.

Once again, there was no one home. The Stones certainly knew how to pick the time in that respect.

I shut the horses in the barn, leaving Free saddled since I was obviously going back, and throwing them monster wedges of hay.

To my relief, my key worked when I tried it in the back door. I went in cautiously, clutching the cloak pin.

At first glance, the kitchen was our familiar farm kitchen. Our huge antique table was square in the centre, and the photo of Mum and Dad on their wedding day stood on the wooden Welsh dresser beneath the shelves of plates and cups.

But the wall clock was different, and there was a lot of stuff missing. The curtains were a cheap check material rather than the amber and green leaf pattern I knew.

It dawned on me that this time layer was very early on in my parents' marriage—before I was born, probably.

I set about my task. No time to waste.

Eothal needed antibiotics and those were beyond my reach— for people. But I was confident penicillin was penicillin whether it was for a sheep or a human, and our farm's veterinary supplies were what I wanted to get my hands on.

I crossed quickly to the farm office. In my own time, the fridge where we kept drugs for the animals was teetering on ancient, so I thought it was likely to be there in this time layer. Mum and Dad always kept animal medicines on hand. Like any farmer, especially with Mum also a veterinary assistant, they had a range of things on hand for animal treatment on the farm.

The fridge was there all right, shiny and new. I had to pass the desk to get to it. I tried not to look, but I caught a glimpse of the big planning diary, open and scribbled in.

I stopped. Rain sputtered against the window.

April, I saw... but the year... I wanted to know. Except that last time when I'd read the year, it triggered the memory switch that almost made me forget Daniel.

What if the cloak pin didn't stop me falling into the wrong memory track this time? I already knew I wasn't in the right year. Why take the risk?

But it was too tempting.

It was three years before I was born. One year before Daniel was born.

My armpits prickled with sweat. I felt the memory shifts beginning in my mind—this time an emptiness trying to force its way in, because I didn't yet exist in this time layer—and gripped the cloak pin like a drowning person snatching at a lifeline.

The cloak pin held firm. The emptiness receded.

I spotted a ball of string on the desk, and I cut a length with a pair of scissors and strung my cloak pin on it. I tied the string round my neck, tucking the cloak pin beneath my clothes so it lay against my skin. I waited, in case my memory failed, but it didn't.

With my hands free, I stepped quickly away from the desk and opened the fridge. Sure enough, a couple of dozen small glass bottles sat on a shelf inside. I located the penicillin and squinted at the tiny printed labels. I needed to work out how many vials to take with me for several days of treatment for Eothal. The doses were for animals, of course, but I guessed Eothal weighed about forty-five kilograms, and the doses had weight ranges with them.

I slid five vials, one each for five days, into a pocket in my backpack.

The penicillin had to be injected, and I needed needles and syringes. I was used to giving jabs. I was Mum's chief helper with all the sick or hurt farm animals.

I checked the clock.

I'd been in the house for twenty minutes – way too long. I could just see Mum and Dad marching in. They'd only be a few years older than me – Mum was twenty-seven when she had me, so she'd be twenty-four in this time layer.

'Hi,' I'd say. 'I look like a thief, but I'm the daughter you'll have in three years.'

And I'd be carted off to some mental institution, and they'd never have me or Daniel after all. Or maybe they would, and this whole thing would just circle around and around in a whirl of time layers.

I opened the drawer where Mum kept sterile syringes, but there were none in it. I searched every drawer in the desk, my hands fumbling and shaking, really sweating now, ears stretched like a deer's, listening for any sound that would warn me some-one was returning.

Finally, I found a stock of syringes in a shoebox on top of the fridge and grabbed a dozen. There was a small glass bottle half-full of paracetamol tablets there too, so I took that. Finally, I picked up a big plastic puffer pack of antibiotic powder from the desk, for applying directly to wounds.

With the whole lot stuffed in my backpack, I hurried back to the kitchen.

As I got there, a car drove into the farmyard.

21

The Keeper of the Stones

I froze, too wiped out by panic to move. There was no other way for me to leave. The kitchen door led right out to where the car was being parked. Luckily I'd locked the door behind me when I came in, to buy some time if anyone arrived.

But it wasn't going to give me much.

The car door slammed, and I turned and bolted through the living room and up the stairs. Daniel's room—or what was going to be Daniel's room—had a tree growing close to the window that was as good as a ladder. We'd both been up and down it often enough. I'd climb down the tree.

I tried to tread silently in the hallway upstairs. It turned out Mum and Dad didn't have carpets in those days and the wooden floorboards complained like old bones. But I made it to Daniel's room and eased the door open. It was completely bare, with whitewashed walls and nothing on the floor apart from a few stacked cardboard boxes.

No carpet in here either, not even a rug to deaden my foot-steps.

Whoever was in the kitchen began running water. Filling the kettle, perhaps. I took advantage of the covering sound to step as lightly and rapidly as possible over to the window.

It was painted shut, the old iron frame spider-webbed. The iron handle that I had to lift was stiff and stuck hard in the locked position. I jabbed at it with the heel of my palm, cursing old houses under my breath.

The noise I was making obscured any sounds from the person in the house, so I couldn't hear where they were.

I paused for a second, feeling for the cloak pin hanging from its string for reassurance, and heard the stairs creaking.

Frantic, I gave the handle a violent noisy whack and knocked it loose. Then I thumped the frame with the side of my fist to break the ancient paint seal. The window popped open and swung wide.

I threw my backpack out first and heard it thump on the ground. I'd hopped up on the sill and out into the tree hundreds of times, and I vaulted up onto the windowsill, hung a leg out, and felt for the big old tree branch with my foot.

Rain swept low and rough across the hills and into my face, and I couldn't feel the branch I needed.

The tree was there, but it was fifteen years smaller than in my own time layer.

I had to jump for it. I crashed through smaller branches and new green leaves and landed on a main branch, a metre below where one was supposed to be. I winded myself, scraped my arms, almost got my eye poked out by a twig. But I was free.

I slithered to the ground, seized my backpack, and ran across the farmyard to the barn, wincing with pain from my ribs and still trying to catch my breath.

'Hey!' a man shouted behind me. 'What d'you think you're doing?'

I didn't know the voice. It had a familiarity, but it wasn't Dad. At the barn door, I glanced back at the house. Beyond the skirts of rain I saw a man at an open bedroom window, not Daniel's but Mum's and Dad's, which didn't have a tree blocking the view. The man was so like Dad that my throat closed and tears sprang into my eyes. But he was older than Dad.

The man vanished from the window and I imagined him hurrying downstairs, perhaps calling the police. I dashed into the barn and got the horses ready, which only took a few moments as I'd left Free saddled. I rode out of the barn and sent Free flying through the open farm gate, towing Molasses alongside her by his lead rope.

They started to race and I let them, steering them out across the nearest pasture, running for the wet woods.

The man had to be my grandfather, Dad's father. He died the year before I was born, so I never met him. Grandma was still alive, although not long after Dad and Mum took over the farm she moved to a cottage in the village. She was still there.

As the horses slowed to walk and the rain stopped, a memory floated into my head.

Mum occasionally told a story about the only burglary we ever had at the farm, a thief who broke in and stole some odds and ends of medicine.

'Grandpa always said he'd have happily given the thief what he needed,' she'd say. 'But it made him really mad that the thief sneaked in.'

The thief was me.

My grandfather had seen me dressed in my Bronze Age woollens and cloak in the wrong time, twelve years old, looking like a boy, three years before I was born. I wished I could explain it to Grandma, who every now and then said what a pity it was that Grandpa didn't live to see me.

But the Stones had made sure he did.

☙☙☙☙☙☙☙

It was dusk when I arrived at the Bull Stones. The horses grazed peacefully, making the most of the good green grass while I waited for it to get dark enough for the moon to angle up into the sky through the ragged clouds so we could cross back into the Bronze Age.

I rested my palm against the Moonstone and felt a vibration, a humming, that told me the Stones recognised me.

Daniel was right about time being in layers. Thousands of invisible layers stacked on top of each other that you could slip between, if you knew how.

And I knew how. I understood the deep magic Tirvold talked about, and the Stones understood me.

Like Tirvold, I was a Keeper of the Stones.

22

The Treatment

Back in the Bronze Age, I turned Free and Molasses loose in the horse pen and hurried to Tirvold's hut to find Eothal. The squalor of the huts struck me anew after my visit to our lovely farmhouse. I'd never thought about it—it was just home, the heart of an ordinary working farm—but it was palatial compared to a Bronze Age hut.

I ducked round the animal skin door-flap and found Tirvold sitting on the floor beside Eothal in the firelight. They were on their own.

I dropped to my knees beside Eothal and touched her forehead. She was burning up again with a dangerous dry fever. Her skin felt as fragile as tissue paper.

'How can she live?' Tirvold said. His hands were twisting another of his small wood carvings and his knife.

'I have medicine,' I said. 'I went through the Stones. It's strong medicine, from my own time.'

Our eyes met. Tirvold's anxious face mirrored the anxiety storming in my blood.

'Will it work?' he said.

'I don't know,' I said, 'but nothing you have works, and it might.'

I scrabbled through the backpack, convulsed with cold. I'd arrived still wet through from the April rain of two years before my birth, and ridden to the village through a Bronze Age winter that bit to the marrow.

I extracted a syringe and a vial of penicillin. Fitted the needle, pierced the top of the vial, tipped it up, and drew the full dose into the syringe with some extra for good measure. Eothal's infection had such a hold on her that I thought I should kick-start the antibiotics with a heavy dose, just like Mum did with our sheep.

I was as certain as I could be that what I was about to inject into Eothal wouldn't kill her, unless she was allergic to it. I had to take that chance. If I didn't try something drastic, she'd die.

If she lived, I'd give her a penicillin jab every morning for four more days.

Which meant I was going to be in the Bronze Age at least another five days, even if I managed to somehow free Daniel from the Long Mound sooner than that.

I thought Tirvold might kill me if Eothal died.

The fire was warming me up. I waited a few more minutes until I'd stopped shaking, since trembling hands weren't good for giving a jab. Then I folded back Eothal's garments to expose her upper arm, and positioned the needle.

'No.' Tirvold seized my wrist.

His tone was one of absolute refusal, and I turned to him in exasperation.

'Tirvold, please,' I said. 'I risked everything to get this, and it might save her life. Nothing else will.'

'You might be trying to kill her,' he said, his desperation evident in his grip on my wrist.

'That doesn't make sense,' I said. 'I don't have to try to kill her. She's going to die anyway. I'm trying to save her.'

Tirvold let go of me and I turned to Eothal. Her eyes were open in her flushed face. Her cracked lips parted.

'Do it,' she whispered.

'See?' I said to Tirvold. 'She trusts me.'

He said nothing. Eothal didn't flinch as I jabbed the needle into her arm and sent the penicillin into her body to start its fight for her life.

I sat for a moment holding the used syringe, watching her, then capped it and tucked it into one of the outside pockets of my backpack so it wouldn't get mixed up with the sterile ones. Then I smiled at Eothal.

'It doesn't work right away,' I said, 'and I need to give you more each day.'

I produced the paracetamol bottle and shook two tablets into my hand. Tirvold watched as I crushed them between stones and brushed the powder into pottery beaker, then half-filled it with water and stirred it around until the particles had more or less dissolved. Eothal was so thirsty that she downed it all without question.

'Those will help to lessen her fever and her pain,' I said to Tirvold. Then I chugged a tablet myself with some water, to help my tree-battered ribs, and Tirvold relaxed. Apparently it made him feel I wasn't poisoning his sister if I could swallow the same stuff. If he'd known how careful Mum had taught me to be with medicine, he wouldn't have worried.

Finally, I uncovered Eothal's Bullwound, washed it, puffed

antibiotic powder onto it, and wrapped it again.

Eothal dropped back into her restless sleep, and gradually the paracetamol took some of the heat out of her.

The next morning Eothal seemed more at ease, and neither she nor Tirvold raised a word of protest when I injected the next penicillin dose and gave her more paracetamol.

In the middle of the afternoon, stiff and sore as I was from my failed tree-climbing adventure, I took Free to the Mound.

I wanted to be near Daniel, to see whether I could feel his presence again.

Under the clouded sky, the snow around the long deathly shape was mashed with bull tracks. The bulls were there, but they kept their distance. In daylight, they didn't seem interested in chasing me. They wanted to stick close to the Mound to protect it and the Bullmaster, I supposed.

But when I ventured closer, I crossed some unmarked line that stirred them into action. They grouped and presented their horns, and I backed off.

I'd seen what they could do with those horns.

I rode a hundred metres away and halted Free near the trees. The bulls, now I'd disturbed them, were fidgety. They trotted about, sparring among themselves.

How could I ever pass them, get into the Mound, and find Daniel?

I'd hoped to see him in one of the visions, or hear him again, but there was nothing to suggest my brother had ever existed.

Betrayal

By the fourth morning, after once again administering penicillin and paracetamol to Eothal, I was convinced she was
going to fully recover.

The fever had left her. The penicillin drove the infection from
the wound and it was healing cleanly. She was able to sit up and
her appetite returned. Tirvold brought her meat, soup, bread,
goat's milk. She devoured it all.

Still nobody except Tirvold knew she was there in the village,
safe and regaining her strength.

The thaw arrived in earnest. The ice-crusted mud and manure
that I crossed as I went about the village melted into sludge, and
the wooden planking the Horse People laid to walk on sank into
it. Everywhere, a stink hung in the air, breaking loose from the
rubbish rotting in the mud.

I wandered aimlessly through the village in thin sunlight,
thinking I might saddle Free and take her and Molasses out to
find a spot where they could graze for a while. The village was
quiet apart from children running about, with most people out
hunting, gathering more wood for fires, repairing buildings, or
tending to their animals.

The short daylight hours provided little time for the tasks

necessary for surviving the winter, and I was ignored. Even Rugal was too busy training horses or working with the other Horse People to spend time with me.

Apart from the brief spells I spent with Tirvold and Eothal, or my nights in the hut with the goats and dogs and fleas and other sleepers, I was alone. Many of the Horse People were sick, laid low by heavy colds, flu, various infections, injuries. Some died, and I'd heard the wailing and seen the quiet lines of people heading to a place outside the village where they cremated their dead. I shied away from the funerals.

I stood near a hut in a patch of chilly sunlight, scratching my side through the layers of wool. I should have stolen some flea powder along with the penicillin.

I had the idea of counting the buildings, thinking that Daniel would be interested in knowing the number. I felt he was slipping beyond my reach, that this might bring him closer again, finding things out for him.

I'd learnt that although there didn't appear to be many huts, sometimes as many as ten people shared them.

The Horse People were mostly hunters, but Tirvold had told us that in spring and summer, they worked on the land some of the time. They grew grain and gathered wild fruit and nuts from the woods, and let their livestock wander. They cut and stored hay for the winter for the horses. The horses grew thin in the winter, though they were able to graze like the sheep and goats when it wasn't snowy.

The hay the horses ate, the villagers cut from long meadow grass on the open land below the hill. It was the same land my family used, three thousand years later, as meadowland for hay.

I discovered a disadvantage to the sheepskin boots. They weren't waterproof.

Voices murmured as I started walking again, counting huts for Daniel. Once I heard a child crying, once somebody laughing. A smell of smoke and cooking meat hung in the air.

I heard shouts from the meeting square.

When I got there, some of the teenage boys were practising dagger fighting with carved pieces of wood. I paused to watch. Two boys, dressed only in wool tunics and leather boots, fenced and lunged while the others watched. When they stopped, one of the men instructing them took the wooden dagger from the taller boy. The boy wiped sweat and dirt from his overheated face and watched as the instructor demonstrated what the boy should have done to kill his opponent. A burst of laughter went up when the victim dropped dramatically to the ground, feigning death.

Another group of villagers was hauling wood into the square and stacking it for the communal fire that night. I thought again of the village I'd been to with Rugal. The Horse People were rough, dirty, and violent, but they had a vibrant grip on life and saw how to make more of themselves. I couldn't imagine them weighed down by the sense of loss and death that oppressed the other village. Its existence seemed doomed.

I left the square, and soon found myself on a small footpath in uncharted territory, my hut count at forty-three so far. No wooden walkway here. I was ankle-deep in mushy snow and rotting rubbish, the slime soaking my boots. I surprised some sheep, but they quickly assumed bored looks as I traipsed past them.

I decided to turn back. I was pretty sure I'd counted every hut. Fifty-eight in all. I'd also counted seventeen rats, two of them dead. Then I heard a voice, and it stopped me in my tracks.

Rugal was speaking in the nearest hut. I didn't catch the words, but it was his voice for sure. I edged closer until I could hear properly.

'What else could I do?' he was saying. He sounded defensive.

'You let them get too far,' a man said.

It was a gravelly voice. Probably Clynwas, Rugal's father and Tirvold's uncle, though I was hazy about how he sounded. It was several days since I'd seen Clynwas, let alone heard him speak.

'The girl was with me,' Rugal said. 'I could not travel at the pace I wanted.'

'But now Eothal has had treatment from the healer,' Clynwas said. 'She may recover.'

I forgot the thaw, forgot Daniel, forgot Tirvold. My body was solid with fear. It was impossible for me to move, not even to lean in closer to hear better or watch and make sure no one saw me.

'She is very sick again,' Rugal was saying, dismissively. 'She will die. There is nothing to fear. A Bullwound always kills.'

A silence, broken by the scrape of something moving or being moved inside the hut.

'He will be angry,' said Clynwas. 'Perhaps this time it will not kill. She has survived longer than anyone.'

If I'd spoken with Rugal in the past few days, if I hadn't heard this, I might have told him about the penicillin. It hurt to breathe. Rugal dropped his voice, but I heard him anyway. There was only a leather door flap between us.

'The Bullmaster will be stronger next time,' he said. 'When there is no moon.'

Daniel had said, your way is wrong.

I wasn't just wrong, but a fool.

Daniel hadn't been talking about the direction I was travelling in, or how far I was from the Bull Stones. He was talking about me placing my trust in Rugal.

Why hadn't he told me in plain words instead of gobbledy-gook code?

And now it might be too late. What did Rugal know that he'd learnt from me?

Muffled footsteps inside the hut sounded like someone might be coming out. I darted away. I had to find Tirvold, and I had to remember what I might have told Rugal that he'd could use against us.

If Daniel was still alive.

It hit me that Daniel's destiny was entwined with Eothal's. I couldn't save Daniel on my own. Tirvold had said Eothal, the queen, could fight the Bullmaster. If she died, there would be no one strong enough to fight the Bullmaster, and I'd never free Daniel. If Eothal died, Daniel might be lost for ever.

Tirvold had used the Stones to seek help, and the Stones had found me. I was their Keeper, as Tirvold was, and the deep magic moved through them to both of us. The Stones had their own power. They inserted me in other time layers when I tried to get home to my own. It was never a time layer that helped me but it was always a time layer that pushed forward Tirvold's goal: defeating the Bullmaster.

I began to think my only chance of getting back to my own time layer with Daniel was if I helped Tirvold and Eothal destroy the Bullmaster's power.

And I had no idea how to do that.

24

An Ancient Feud

I arrived at Tirvold's hut a short time later. He was sitting on the floor, leaning against the wall in the company of a couple of snoozing goats while he carved another small wooden animal. He pointed to Eothal and put his finger to his lips when I entered.

I nodded and stepped up to Eothal's bed.

She lay curled on her side with a woollen blanket over her, fast asleep and breathing softly. I laid the back of a finger on her forehead—no fever. It would be time for more paracetamol in an hour or so, but I decided I wouldn't wake her.

I'd done it. I'd saved Eothal's life. I was Lizzie Brave the healer.

Tirvold told me in a low voice that I should eat, which I'd completely forgotten to do. There was something bubbling over the fire in a metal pot, soup or stew. I scooped a wooden bowlful—it was amazing how I no longer cared that they never washed the bowls—and lifted it to my mouth. It was thick with barley and shreds of mutton.

I burnt my mouth and my throat, slurping like a wolf pup. I managed to eat a refill in a more civilised fashion. Not that table manners meant anything around here.

'Your medicine is good,' Tirvold said, quietly. 'Our father died of such a Bullwound, and others too have died. Slow deaths, painful deaths that make you weep to remember them.'

'She needs one more dose of medicine,' I said, 'but I think she'll get better.'

Tirvold smiled, and it jolted me hard. It could have been Daniel smiling at me.

'And she can sleep,' Tirvold said. 'A Bullwound burns the soul as well as the flesh, and fills dreams with terrors. Your medicine has vanquished that too.'

I tipped up my bowl, sucking the last drops, then put it back on a shelf, unwiped. I was so at home in the Bronze Age these days.

'Now will you help me get Daniel out of the Mound?' I asked.

Tirvold owed me. I'd saved his sister. He had to help me save my brother. But he shook his head reluctantly.

'I have never known the Mound open for any but the Bull-master,' he said.

But I knew how to open the Endstones, even though I hadn't told anyone yet.

'But they used to bury people there... your ancestors,' I said. 'Don't the Horse People know how to get in?'

'The secret is lost,' he said.

I thought of the archaeologist's explanation. If there was only some way of getting rid of the bulls, I could try it. Look for the levers that rolled the Endstones open.

Rugal had said it was magic. Either he believed it himself, or he wanted me to believe it.

'Tirvold,' I said, 'I think Rugal's working for the Bullmaster.'

Tirvold got up and dipped his bread in the pot over the fire, bit off the dunked section, and stared at me with Daniel's eyes.

'I feared it was so,' he said.

'Why didn't you tell me?' I said, trying to control my anger.

'You would not have believed me,' Tirvold said. 'He helped you and you liked him and resented me.'

'I'm sorry,' I said. Tirvold sat down again and pointed at me with his piece of bread.

'How do you feel about him now?' he asked.

I stared back at him. 'Afraid.'

'But you must keep behaving as if you trust him,' Tirvold said. 'If he suspects, he will bring the Bullmaster upon us immediately, before Eothal is ready, and all will be lost.'

'But why hasn't he done that already?' I asked.

'Because the Bullmaster is waiting to be sure Eothal, the last of the queens, is dead,' Tirvold said. 'Then the Horse People will be without a queen.'

I wondered again if Daniel even knew how the Stones worked. He wasn't a Keeper. I told Tirvold how the Stones vibrated under my hand, and he nodded. It was the deep magic, he said, that marked me as the Keeper of the Stones.

'You are the Keeper of the Stones in your time,' Tirvold said. 'They know this.'

And that put me in danger too.

Rugal must have worked out by now that I was a Keeper. Perhaps the Bullmaster would keep Daniel alive to use as bait to trap me. Tirvold and I were both targets.

Whatever I did, I couldn't make Rugal suspicious, because if he really was working with the Bullmaster he would tell him, and the Bullmaster would kill Daniel and come for me.

Tirvold had finished eating and his hands were busy with another wood carving.

'Eothal tried to warn me, but I didn't listen,' I said. Even Daniel had tried to warn me. Your way is wrong.

'The Bullmaster will not wait if he learns Eothal is recovering,' Tirvold said. 'He will attack now, while she is still weak. Does Rugal know about your medicine?'

'No,' I said. I bit my lip, not wanting to admit that was only a matter of luck.

'That's good,' Tirvold said. 'The Bullmaster expects her to die, and soon. He will wait for that. If she died, Rugal and Clynwas would tell the village to give me up to save themselves.'

He got up and helped himself to a bowl of stew, and in the silence I remembered that Tirvold was the one who had arranged for Daniel to be taken by the Bullmaster, to buy himself some time or maybe save himself entirely.

There was nothing clear-cut here. Even what now appeared certain about Rugal might have an explanation.

The only person I could trust was myself.

❧ ❧ ❧ ❧ ❧ ❧

Later, when Eothal stirred, I gave her more paracetamol. Her wound was almost perfectly healed. Her eyes bright in the firelight, she downed two hearty bowls of the mutton stew, chattering with Tirvold the whole time.

The fire had burnt down to embers and the hut was getting dark. Tirvold set about feeding the dying flames with wood from the stack near the doorway.

'Tirvold,' I said. 'Did you know we might be related?'

He grinned. 'I was thinking so,' he said.

Together, we unwound the threads. My last name, Greenwood. My ability to ride like the Horse People. Daniel being the spitting image of Tirvold even though he couldn't ride like the Horse People (or anyone, really). Tirvold and me, both of us the Keepers of the Stones, each in our own time layer.

We didn't mention my red hair, so like Rugal's.

Eventually, I gave myself up to the exhaustion that had been crushing me for hours, stretched out on the floor by their fire, and slept there for the night instead of going back to my own hut and my friends the goats.

એ_૭ એ_૭ એ_૭ એ_૭ એ_૭ એ_૭

In the morning, in frosty air that made our breath circle our faces like smoke, I gave Eothal the fifth and final jab of penicillin. I handed her the puffer bottle of antibiotic powder and told her to keep it.

I had a feeling that now she was so much better, she'd vanish again, and she could apply that herself until the wound was completely healed.

Tirvold and I each milked a goat and we all three drank the warm foamy milk and chewed on hard bread, squatting on the floor around the small fire in the middle of the hut. Tirvold rebuilt it again, the flames licking up the new branches as he added them. Starting a fire was hard work and the Horse People tried to keep them going all winter.

I would have given almost anything for a breakfast of bacon and eggs back in my own time layer. Real toast with butter and jam.

After we'd finished eating, Eothal began to move about the hut, testing her strength and gathering items she might need for the next couple of days. Food, furs, weapons.

Tirvold pushed his fingers through his long dark hair, then produced one of his wooden animals and shaved away with his knife.

'You could have used the medicine to bargain,' he said.

'Bargain?' I said.

'Yes. You could have said you would not treat Eothal unless we helped you try to save your brother.'

Why didn't I think of that? All along, I'd thought of things too late — or not at all.

Tirvold inspected his latest carving, a sheep.

'I thank you that you did not,' he said seriously.

He paused, and somehow I expected he'd go on to say that he was so grateful to me for possibly saving the life of his sister that he'd do anything to help me crack the Mound open and rescue my brother.

But what he did was get up and leave the hut with Eothal, and I didn't see them again for days.

25

The Fox

Over the next couple of days, I rode to the Long Mound several times. The bulls appeared each time I reached it and kept me at a distance.

I was sure now that Daniel was still alive, but what sort of state could he be in, after so long underground in the darkness of the great tomb?

I kept up my visits to the horse pens, as I'd agreed with Tirvold. I sought out Rugal and talked to him as though everything was normal, and rode with him when he hunted.

Despite everything, I loved to watch him train the horses, teaching them manners, obedience, respect. They learnt to follow him at a distance of a metre or so, stopping when he did, backing up when he backed, turning, standing, lifting their legs at one touch when he wanted to clean their feet with his bronze pick.

He rode them bareback, bending them around his legs, teaching them to work with relaxed, curved necks, balanced and ultra responsive.

Each day Rugal rode Free and Molasses too, and taught them what he was teaching the others. He seemed to have horse blood in his veins. He rode a horse the way a hawk rode the wind.

He loved each horse, and gradually I gave way again to what

I'd always believed, that someone who loved horses couldn't be bad.

I couldn't carry on believing that he was truly in league with the Bullmaster. Maybe his father Clynwas was, and Rugal was only pretending. After all, he hadn't done what Clynwas had wanted. Clynwas had been angry with him when I overheard them. Rugal had been making excuses.

I believed I was wrong and Tirvold was wrong — and that Rugal was on my side, not the Bullmaster's.

Tirvold and Eothal had disappeared again, still not helping me with saving Daniel, whereas Rugal talked about that often. He rode with me to the Long Mound and tried to help me plan the rescue of my brother.

I desperately needed help. Still, I was more cautious. We talked about horses and Daniel. I answered questions Rugal had about my own time. But I avoided talking about the Stones or Eothal, or even Tirvold. And I never, ever mentioned the End-stones.

ᕦᑐ ᕦᑐ ᕦᑐ ᕦᑐ ᕦᑐ ᕦᑐ

One afternoon I rode with Rugal across the hills to inspect the wild horse herds that the Horse People claimed as their own. Some of the horses were trained already. The Horse People released them to run in herds and fend for themselves, catching them to ride when they needed them to go hunting.

Rugal trained the best horses in more advanced work for several weeks at a time, and during that period he kept them in the pens. After that they were sold. But that trade was dwindling. At one time, people had travelled from far-flung villages to buy horses, but the Bullmaster had destroyed too many and now almost nobody came.

A few men still did. But when I saw these men, they were quiet and grey like the men I'd seen in the village with the death-stench, and it chilled me to the core.

Rugal regularly checked the herds for injured, sick, or missing animals. The horses stayed in the area, or wandered and came back, because the Horse People put out hay for them when it snowed — not a lot, but enough to hold their loyalty.

The difference Rugal's training had brought about in Free was amazing. She strode out beneath me, her head relaxed and low, her neck arched. She was attentive, understanding that I was in charge and waiting for me to tell her what I wanted. She was soft in my hands and responded instantly to the lightest touch from the reins or my heels.

So I rode through the chilly, damp day with a furtive grin on my face.

We rounded a belt of forest — there was so much more forest in the Bronze Age time layer than in my own time layer, the Bronze Age forest teeming with birds and deer — and made for a small horse band led by a grey stallion. They were some way off, grazing between the disappearing snow patches.

A big dog fox crossed the open land in a leisurely trot, trailing a heavy white-tipped brush. The fox was almost the same colour as Rugal's hair or my hair, vivid as a flame in the winter monochrome. Farther away, red deer grazed. Hearing us, they lifted their heads and then slipped into the edge of the wood. The clouds bunched low on the horizon in tired, ill-formed heaps.

'How is Eothal?' Rugal asked.

It was out of the blue. Neither of us had said anything for the past few minutes.

My eyes and nostrils dilated with panic but I caught it fast, controlling my face. When I looked at him, he wasn't looking at me. He was watching the fox.

'I don't know anything about Eothal,' I said.

'I see,' he said.

I had to know.

'Rugal,' I said. 'I heard you a few days ago. Talking to Clynwas about the Bullmaster.'

Now he looked at me, sharply. 'Where?'

I told him I'd been walking between the huts and their voices had reached me. Rugal shrugged.

'My father goes off on his own track sometimes,' he said. 'Everyone worries about the Bullmaster, the best way to manage him.'

He reined in Sostis and turned the horse to face me. His green eyes burned beneath his red hair. The gold ring glinted at his throat.

'The Horse People are my people,' Rugal said. 'My father rants and raves. But how could I give my people into death and slavery?'

'It didn't sound like that,' I said. I wondered if I'd gone too far. Tirvold had said to keep Rugal believing I felt safe with him.

'Lizzie Brave,' Rugal said. 'My father is tempted. He is old and he fears the Bullmaster. But I am not my father.'

I looked away. The fox, sitting bolt upright, watched us with his black-tipped ears triangled. His mouth opened and his tongue looped pink as he yawned. He was a beautiful fox.

'So what do you think?' I said.

'For now, I am letting my father believe I too follow the Bull-master,' Rugal said. 'That way, he will keep talking to me and I can prevent disaster. If you do not trust me, consider what happened when we tracked Tirvold and Eothal. At any time I could have led the Bullmaster to them, but I did not.'

Could he have done? Maybe he could, maybe not. But it was true that he hadn't. Rugal surveyed the land in front of us, no longer covered in snow. Most of it had melted, leaving a few drab patches like white scabs on the grey-green grass beneath.

It was Tirvold who had left Daniel to be caught by the Bull-master, not Rugal. Rugal was helping me. How could I take Tir-vold's word over his? I bit my lower lip and nodded.

'So, if you have seen Eothal,' he continued. 'Is she better?'

I breathed deep, stepped over the edge. No harm in answering the question if he was against the Bullmaster. He wasn't asking where she was. And if he told Clynwas she was better, maybe that would stop Clynwas worrying about the Bullmaster.

I told Rugal I hadn't seen Eothal or Tirvold for a few days. That I'd brought her medicine from my own time and she was healing, the last time I saw her.

Rugal nodded. 'My father will be happy to hear that,' he said.

But he didn't look at me, and he turned his horse with a hard kick that wasn't necessary — Sostis flinched beneath it, surprised.

Too late, I remembered Tirvold saying that if the Bullmaster thought Eothal was recovering, he would attack before she could get really well.

But I crushed the tiny moth of doubt that fluttered inside me before it could spread its wings and choke me with fear.

We rode on and approached the horse herd. The grey stallion smelt us from a hundred metres away in big snorts, his attention on Rugal's stallion Sostis. Then he rounded up his mares and sent them running up a hill flank. We watched them go, all sound, ribs showing on a few of them, but not too bad.

'The young ones I will catch and train this spring, and we will trade or sell them later,' Rugal said. The sun wriggled through the loose cloud coverlet, casting a pallid light over the landscape as we turned back towards the village.

'Who owns those horses?' I said.

'A few belong to the Horse People, but most belong to Eothal and Tirvold,' Rugal said. 'They are royal horses. I train them, and they sell them.'

A pause, in which a hawk called, thin and high.

'Do they pay you?' I asked.

'Not with gold,' he said. 'I can choose one for myself from each season to sell or keep. One horse each year out of the hundreds they have. But it cannot be the one they judge to be the best.'

Rugal didn't sound as though he liked the arrangement.

'Is that how you got Sostis?' I asked.

'Yes,' he said, 'from the former queen.'

A small cold smile lay briefly on his face, a flicker of triumph.

'It was a misjudgement on her part,' he said. 'He is truly a great horse.'

I understood why Rugal wasn't happy. He was right. It wasn't a fair arrangement. And this, I realised, was the greed feud   Tirvold had talked about. And maybe it was enough to push Rugal to want the Bullmaster to win.

26

The Battle Begins

I struggled in a dream about Daniel, enveloped in sleep and unable to push my way out. All around me were the noises of running feet, low cries of fear, dogs barking.

A child shrieking.

That finally tore me free of the dream, and I sat up in the hut. The fire was out, the light the muted colour of its ashes. Morning, but still early, and something was going on.

The hut was empty. Even the goats had vanished. I flung off my blanket and wolfskins and bolted outside (like everyone else, I slept in all my clothes), battering the leather flap aside and running smack into a villager, his brown eyes set hard in his lined face.

Our collision knocked him a little off stride, but he ran on without speaking, his feet thumping on the planks.

'What's happening?' I yelled after him.

From all over the village I heard people running along the wood walkways, some shouting orders. A low hoarse yell from somewhere near the main gate by the causeway sent chills through me. I stood on the path, buffeted by people scurrying in all directions, falling off the planks into the mud in their panic. Some carried food, others bundles, children, firewood, swords and armour.

A man I knew by sight walked rapidly by, towing three horses behind him by the reins. More hooves followed, and I saw Rugal on his red stallion.

'Rugal!' I shouted.

Reaching him, I stood shivering in a cold fine drizzle that had just begun. He looked down, his expression hard.

'The Bullmaster is preparing to attack,' he said. 'You should flee. A battle is no place for you.'

He sent his horse forward through the throng.

No calling me Lizzie Brave now. No request for help.

I hurried on, alone.

A band of men and women were reinforcing the palisade fence. Others were deepening the big ditch with bronze-bladed tools. Children herded the farm animals into groups and crowded them into the stock pens.

Men and women arrived from outside with horses caught from the roaming herds, presumably for the warriors to ride into battle.

Rugal was right to tell me I had no place here. Everyone else knew what to do, and I had no idea. I was useless. And fighting in a battle? Me? I wasn't Joan of Arc.

Campfire smoke rose from the surrounding hills. Bands of men had gathered some distance off. I wondered if they were from the conquered villages, people forced now to fight for the Bullmaster.

Not people—men. All their women and children dead, if the empty village I'd visited with Rugal was an example of what the Bullmaster did.

Or maybe the Bullmaster had lured his wasted army with the promise of gold, in this, the richest village. The Horse People's wealth was built on the horses Rugal and Clynwas trained, riding into a new world, and no other village around here had that kind of wealth.

Afraid that Free might have been seized for use as a warhorse, I ran for the horse pens, forcing my way through the people around me, my feet thudding on wooden walkways slippery with mud.

The men had taken all the other horses, but not my two. I saddled and mounted Free. I was afraid to leave Molasses on his own so I led him at my side as I rode, heading for the village square.

For once, Free's pricked ears and springy stride had no power to soothe me.

I needed to find Rugal again.

My stomach snarled with panic. What if I'd got it wrong? What if Rugal was a traitor?

'He can't be,' I said to Free.

My hand twisted in her mane, but I stopped as soon as I realised what I was doing. I had to get myself under control.

Tirvold had told me that if the Bullmaster found out that Eothal was recovering, he'd try to attack before she was well enough to really stand up to him. I'd told Rugal she was getting better just yesterday, and now the Bullmaster was preparing an attack.

Maybe it wasn't him. Maybe he'd told Clynwas, and Clynwas had contacted the Bullmaster. But a sick feeling tightened my stomach as the fear grew that I might be the one who triggered the destruction of the village.

That after all, the village was going to be found burned and dead by the archaeologists in my time layer, because of me.

I stopped a young woman hurrying by with a baby in her arms, so wrapped in rain-dewed wool he might have been a lamb.

'Is the Bullmaster coming?' I asked timidly.

The woman looked up at me through wet strings of brown hair, her blue eyes sliding between panic and an urge to impart information.

'They say he is,' she said. 'Now we will die under him like the others.'

Panic took over. She hugged her baby, tears rushing down her face.

'The Queen will defeat him,' I said, not knowing what else to say.

'She is not here,' wailed the woman. 'They say she is dead.'

I sat on my horse in the drizzle, watching her stumble away in the mud.

Tirvold had told me not to trust Rugal. Even Daniel had told me in that veiled sentence. Your way is wrong.

I had overheard Rugal myself, in his hut with his father.

Yet I'd still convinced myself that Rugal was all right, because he was an incredible horseman and I admired that so much that I suppressed everything else.

Because he told me he wasn't on the side of the Bullmaster and I wanted to believe him.

Because it was Tirvold who arranged for Daniel's capture.

Because I was lost without Daniel, afraid to be on my own,

and let myself be led by the only person who seemed prepared to look after me.

In the cold rain, these excuses sounded so weak I couldn't believe how I'd fooled myself. What had I done? How had I not seen it? Rugal was ambitious, the best horse trainer of the Horse People, the best hunter, the best rider. The village wealth was built on the horses that Rugal trained, but Eothal and Tirvold owned most of them. Rugal wasn't getting what he deserved.

His family wanted gold. They had watched the queen — three queens — grow in wealth that he made possible.

That led to the greed-feud. And the greed feud led to the Bullmaster.

Rugal had told me that the Bullmaster promised safe passage to those who chose to follow him. Rugal had taken me to the dead village, and he'd been treated like royalty.

It had to be because he had connections with the Bullmaster. Rugal must have gone to the village partly to check up on how things were going, maybe to set in motion preparations for battle, a battle against his own people.

Maybe he'd been missing in the night because he'd been reporting to the Bullmaster.

Rugal hadn't worried at all about what I might see there. Which meant he thought I was so inconsequential, so low down as a possible threat, that I didn't matter.

The thought both mortified me and made me furious.

And what about when I went to the Mound? When I'd gone on my own, the bulls had always been there to stop me. The one time I was able to reach it after Daniel was captured, Rugal was with me.

What had I been thinking? Even now, I still hoped this wasn't the way it was going to turn out. Not just because it destroyed my belief in him, but because it meant I was in it with him, that I'd made things worse.

I'd helped the Bullmaster. He might now be only hours from crushing this village, killing the women and children. Turning it into a place like the one where I'd spent the night. Or destroying it entirely.

What if Daniel was dead, and somehow I'd contributed?

What if I got killed?

I kicked Free and she shot forward with a protesting grunt, Molasses trotting after her at the end of the lead rope. At the square, I found Rugal mounted on Sostis, shouting directions to a number of men with horses. He seemed to be in charge of who should have which animal. Sostis was sweating and steaming in the chilly drizzle. The reins were draped, loose on his neck. Rugal had both hands free and was controlling his horse with balance and knees alone.

My stomach knotted and unknotted and knotted again as I watched.

Rugal saw me and signalled me to stop with one raised hand. I halted and waited on Free, holding Molasses quiet beside us, and tried to get my insides under control while Rugal rode over to me.

I didn't care any more about the danger I might be in.

'You told him, didn't you?' I said furiously.

He knew what I meant. He gazed at me, his eyes soft as moss, but unreadable.

'You think I am part of the forces of the Bullmaster?' he asked.

I nodded.

'Tirvold has told you this?'

'Yes,' I said. 'He said if the Bullmaster knew Eothal was getting better, he'd attack, and not wait to learn about the Stones.'

A silence. Rugal shrugged.

'So how does that involve me?' he said.

I twisted a few strands of Free's mane.

'Yesterday I told you she was getting better, and today the Bullmaster is ready to fight,' I said, 'and Eothal has disappeared.'

Rugal's horse moved its head, and he corrected it with cold anger.

'And where is Tirvold?' he said, his voice as icy as the rain.

'I haven't seen him for days,' I admitted.

'So,' Rugal said. 'Tirvold is not in the village, and I am, and you think it is me who told the Bullmaster?'

He had a point. If he were on the Bullmaster's side, wouldn't he be out there with him? I was so used to Tirvold disappearing that I hadn't even thought about what it could mean.

Rugal gave me a scornful look. He picked up the reins and Sostis stepped back. Rugal wheeled him on the spot and rode off. Free and Molasses wanted to follow, but I held them motionless in the rain.

☙☙☙☙☙☙☙

All day the Horse People prepared for siege and battle while showers of black rain squalled around them. They knew the Bullmaster would not attack before dark.

I went back to my sleeping hut. It was empty apart from the goats, who seemed pleased to see me, unaware of approaching disasters.

The Bullmaster killed all women and children.

I was going to die.

I was going to die in a battle or a fire. Daniel was going to die in the Mound. How had I ever believed it would be otherwise? How had we become caught up in this awful mess, nothing to do with us, not even our time layer?

I yelled, 'Why? Why me?'

It alarmed the goats and they scattered, leaving me alone in the hut.

When I ventured outside again, the village was calmer. The Horse People were in the last stages of preparations for battle and an acceptance of the situation seemed to have taken over.

I ran into Rugal at the horse pens.

'There's going to be a fire,' I said dully. 'She found my cloak pin.'

Rugal had no idea what I was babbling about.

'Lizzie, you have done all you can,' he said. 'You cannot save your brother by remaining here. You will die in this battle. Tonight you must go back to your own time and save yourself.'

If I went back, my memories of Daniel would be swallowed up in some alternative future, so I'd never know. Was that better than death?

What if I died here, in the fire, leaving only my cloak pin for an archaeologist to discover? I'd seen the different time layers and how they worked. Mum and Dad would never know they'd had us. Nobody would miss me.

But I'd still be dead.

I said nothing, and Rugal mounted his horse and left. I took

Free but shut Molasses in the pen with a heap of dry grass. I pressed my face into his black shaggy neck and breathed in his horse scent.

'Goodbye,' I whispered. 'They're Horse People. They'll look after you.'

I didn't see how I could take Molasses back with me. If I was right in choosing a time layer that had never known Daniel, Molasses probably wouldn't exist in that time layer either.

Then I mounted Free and left.

I would ride to the Stones and go home, to a time layer I didn't want to be in, and try to forget I ever had a brother. I didn't know what else I could do.

I wanted to live too much.

Return of the Queen

By early evening, the rain had passed on. Wet cloud remained, shrouding the hilltops. A thin wind licked the temperature low enough to be grindingly cold. A few fading snow patches clung to the ground.

The village was ready, the fence and ditch reinforced and patrolled, the people armed and mounted and waiting. But Eothal had not appeared, and fear rattled through the waiting groups.

As dusk fell I rode Free along the slush-covered pathways, trying to stay invisible. At least we'd be going back to my real life.

And if I left the cloak pin behind, I'd forget all this had ever happened. But I still had it with me, on the string round my neck. I wasn't quite ready to be that final.

I'd be abandoning Daniel, but I could count on my memories being replaced by different time layer memories—of me as an only child.

I'd tried my hardest. I didn't know what more I could do.

Free turned an ear my way as we trotted towards the main gate. The wind softened and brushed us and the sky, teasing the clouds into rags. The moon hadn't risen yet.

It wouldn't take long to get to the Stones.

I'd pass through for the final time.

I'd be home.

Before I reached the gate, a shout went up. The people around me stirred and their voices rose in a wave as they surged along the pathways toward the central square. Dozens of running feet thudded on the walkway planks.

The muttering swelled to cheering.

I checked Free and turned her, following the Horse People. I rode into the square with a clear view over the heads of the crowd from my elevated position on horseback.

At the centre of the square, Eothal shone as brightly as a star. She rode a new horse, a mouse-grey stallion that looked blue in the translucent rain-polished light of the evening.

Now that she was well, she rode the way Rugal rode, the way Rugal said I rode. One fluid movement away from being a centaur.

Eothal was in full armour, a sword at her hip, a spear in her raised hand.

'Tonight I am whole again,' she said.

Her voice was strong and deep, filled with pride and courage, and carried easily over the crowd.

'Tonight the Bullmaster meets his destroyer,' she said. 'From tonight, the Horse People will be a free people, and the villages he conquered will also be free.'

The square was rammed with people. There must only have been a few guards left at the fence protecting the village.

All around Eothal, the cheering grew, and her blue stallion pinned back his ears and reared. Her body flowed with his. She checked him with one hand. He dropped to the ground again and stood trembling with his eyes bulging and his neck a steel

coil, flattening his ears against the cheers and singing of the villagers.

'Listen to me, my people,' Eothal said.

Her voice flew effortlessly across the square and the Horse People fell silent. I realised my mouth was open and closed it, with a sideways glance in case anyone had noticed.

It was a shock to see Rugal on his horse at the edge of the crowd. He was transfixed by Eothal's presence, like the rest of us.

'We will ride to meet the Bullmaster,' Eothal said. 'I will strike him before he knows he is facing his doom, as our former queen did before me. The power of the Moon is not his. The power of the Moon is mine.'

The blue stallion was motionless now, his head raised and his ears pricked. He was listening, like the rest of us, to that triumphant musical voice.

'Fear is our weapon,' Eothal said. 'He has honed our fear and we will take it up to wield it, sharp and strong, against him. He tried to deal death to me, but he dealt life.'

It was me that dealt life to Eothal. Me and the antibiotics I stole from my family before I was born. But that wouldn't have sounded as good in a rallying speech, so I told myself to let it go.

'And now he knows that even his bulls cannot destroy me,' Eothal said.

A roar, a full-throated cheer, thundered around me. Her words and the response lifted me out of my pit of despair.

All my belief that I could save Daniel came flooding back.

I must be feeling the same charge of hope and power that

Eothal, the queen, had sent rushing into the Horse People. I whipped around, looking for Rugal, and glimpsed his red hair vanishing into the dark.

I turned back to take one last look at Eothal. Another figure on a horse stepped up beside her. It was Tirvold on his dun horse, Deer.

As if he felt my gaze land on him, Tirvold glanced across the square and looked straight at me.

We stared at each other and it was as though the deep magic surged between us.

We were the Keepers of the Stones, Tirvold and I.

Finally, I knew what I had to do.

28

Time to Ride

As night fell, the wind ripped the last fragments of cloud from the sky like pieces of velvet, leaving it polished and dark and filling with stars. A new moon was rising, as cold and white as an ice carving.

The Horse People gathered, singing a fierce song of war, at the gate to the village.

I wanted to speak to Tirvold and jumped off Free. It was easier to lead her through the crowd than try to ride. Everyone was armed, and I bumped into spears and swords and hard armour as I pushed through the press of people.

Tirvold, his face burnished by torchlight, was still astride Deer and singing with the rest of them. Beside him Eothal was silent, serene and terrible on her blue-grey stallion.

I reached up and snatched at Tirvold's cloak, feeling like a toddler.

'Tirvold,' I said, 'will you help me?'

Because I understood that if I left the Bronze Age purely to save myself, and in doing so left my brother to die, no amount of magic would stop me knowing, somewhere inside myself, that I had chosen the coward's path.

Your way is wrong, Daniel had said.

Tirvold stared down at me, unsmiling. But when he spoke, I realised he wasn't intentionally shutting me out. His voice was full of regret.

'Lizzie Brave, I know of no way to free your brother, if he is even still alive,' he said. 'The bulls let no one tread the way of the Mound.'

He'd called me Lizzie Brave.

'Can't you kill the bulls?' I pleaded. 'There are so many of you.'

'My father tried to kill them, and died himself from the Bull-wound,' Tirvold said. 'Then my sister Eothal was gored.'

'But Eothal didn't die,' I said.

Eothal heard her name and her gaze landed on me like a bird of prey.

'No, for you saved me,' she said, 'and I owe you a blood-debt. But even I cannot part the Mound and save your brother. My destiny lies with the Bullmaster alone, and if I am the victor, it may be that the Mound can be entered and your brother uncovered.'

Or maybe the bulls would guard it for ever. Or maybe not.

An idea sprang like fire into my mind, an idea that would have made Daniel proud, with his layers of time.

The horses were moving, the people gathering themselves to ride out and fight. Rank upon rank of them, armed with spears, swords, knives, axes.

Rugal, the great archer, the great horseman, was strangely absent.

Eothal and Tirvold turned their horses away from me and rode out to lead the Horse People into battle.

I stepped aside and watched them stream away in the gloom.

Their fierce singing, a shouted, fighting chant, rode with them on the wind. This was my chance.

If the Bullmaster was engaged in battle with Eothal, surely he would have the bulls with him too. They wouldn't be guarding the Mound. So if I got in, and if I endured the dark, I could get Daniel out. If he was still alive.

But even if the bulls were there, I had a plan for them — though it terrified me almost more than the idea of crawling inside that dark tomb in search of my brother.

I leant against Free's furry neck, taking deep breaths. She stood patiently, then turned her head questioningly. I gave her a rub between the eyes and she dipped her head. She was so calm, so peaceful.

But then she had no idea what lay in front of us.

If I kept thinking about it, I'd give up again.

I put a foot in the stirrup and landed soft and light in the saddle. One squeeze of my calves and she moved off, responsive and alert the way Rugal had trained her, making me feel better just because my horse and I were together.

She shied a little at a burning torch someone had left stuck in a pile of soil near the fence. I edged her close enough to grab it. If I took light into the Mound, I would have a defence against the dark.

I rode down the hill from the village, following the broad slippery track of mud and ragged melting slush left by the warrior horde. Free slid down part of it on her haunches. The flaming torch in my hand made her anxious, and at the bottom of the slope I let her break into a canter.

A storm of shouting broke out to one side of me. Screams too, and a clanging of metal on metal. A fight, the first of the battle. A loose horse broke from the knot and galloped past me. Free, already trying to speed up in the belief that she could outrun the fire I carried, bucked explosively.

I stayed on and got her under control but I dropped the torch. I hauled her up, dismounted, and picked it up still burning. But Free seemed to have forgotten all her training. She ran round me in circles as I tried to mount with the burning torch in one hand.

Out of the corner of one eye, I saw a shape that could have been a bull.

Even with Free running about, I managed to thrust my foot in the stirrup and claw myself into the saddle one-handed. She galloped off before I was properly seated, but somehow I settled on her back anyway, my torch still burning.

Free was flying back to the village, whinnying for the horse that had passed her, now long gone in the night. I turned her and sent her on a wide circle around the battlefield, to reach the Mound beyond.

One by one, the bulls peeled away from the fight and followed me. I knew it was useless, but I tossed away the torch in the vain hope that it would make me harder to track. Maybe they'd lose me.

Not a chance.

The bulls, even sightless, could hear me and smell me, and I had no doubt they knew exactly where I was going anyway. They'd probably beat me there.

But it encouraged me. If the Bullmaster wanted the bulls to stop me getting to the Mound, Daniel must still be alive.

There was not a shred of hope that I'd be able to reach the Long Mound, find the lever, open the doors, and search for Daniel before the bulls gored me to death. Even if I did some-how manage it, they'd kill Daniel and me when we reappeared.

I had to forget the Mound and make my back-up plan work. And as the Keeper of the Stones, I thought I could do it.

With the bulls pursuing me, I turned Free and set her gallop-ing for the Stone Circles.

29

The Legend of the Bull Stones

Using the Stones and their power was my one chance to get rid of the bulls. When I needed antibiotics for Eothal, the Stones had taken me to a time layer where I could get them. Now I had to make the deep magic work to take me to the seventeenth century.

If I pulled it off, I'd invent the legend of the Bull Stones. If I didn't, I'd end up somewhere else.

Or maybe dead.

But I'd created the story in my family about the medicine thief. And now I was determined to give the Bull Stones their name. I'd lead the bulls into the seventeenth century and leave them there, and I'd come back and rescue Daniel.

Free galloped over the snow-blotched ground with the bulls relentlessly churning behind us. She was using every ounce of her desert-bred Arabian speed, sweat soaking her neck and making the reins slippery. With the snow largely melted, the going was easier for her and she was faster than the bulls, but we were heading uphill and it was hard for her to keep up her pace.

The Stone Circles glimmered above us in the light spilling from the half-shell of the rising moon. The ground became steeper. When I looked back, the bulls were closer.

The leader was in front with its bronze curved horns, the others charging behind it, running fast enough to gain on me with every stride.

I looked over my shoulder straight into the sightless eye sockets of the lead bull. Ten metres lay between us, and it seemed content to follow more slowly. The bulls believed I couldn't escape, that they could take their time.

Behind the lead bull, the others rippled over the thawing ground, the tilted moon creeping up the sky over their backs. At any moment, I was sure, they'd charge. And I had to wait for it. I needed to take them with me.

I was holding Free together, talking to her and urging her on through her exhaustion. She took uneven, jelly-like strides, her heartbeat hammering through the saddle into my own body. Even as we crested the hill and I checked the position of the moon—right where I needed it—I was afraid she would collapse beneath me.

She stumbled and I felt her front legs starting to fold.

The lead bull sensed it too. He surged up the last slope with his back bent like a bow. The others streamed behind him in a V formation.

I was going to die after all, before I could get through the Stones.

I shouted at Free, pounding her ribs with my heels, and the bronze-horned bull bellowed in victory. I found the moon floating in a sky lacerated with stars… and we stepped into a summer afternoon.

Thick grass, bursting with insects, softened my landing as Free's legs buckled and I tumbled off. Below us the fields

stretched out, not very different from my own time. Away down the slopes, I saw a farm where our farmhouse now was.

Had I come to the wrong time layer?

The drumming of the bulls' hooves filled my ears.

They flashed by us. Bewildered by the strong sunshine, which seemed to sap their power even though they were blind, they no longer paid us any attention. Their momentum sent them down the hill through rich meadow grass emblazoned with flowers. The air filled with flocks of butterflies, taking flight in their thousands as the bulls hammered by.

The fields below were busy with people working, scything hay and gathering crops. They were dressed in the sort of farm worker garb I'd hoped to see – seventeenth century clothes: smocks, loose shirts, clogs or bare feet.

I was in the right time layer.

The farmworkers threw down tools that to me looked old-fashioned and hand-made. They ran about, pointing, yelling, running. Hats flew off.

The bulls gathered at the bottom of the hill in an uneasy clump.

❧❧❧❧❧❧❧

I turned back to my horse and to planning my next steps. Free had recovered her breath. I took hold of the reins and she lurched to her feet and gazed at me, dripping with sweat.

In a moment I'd take her to find water, but first I had to get rid of some clothes. It felt like a hot August afternoon, the air humming with heat and alive with far more insects than in my own time layer — butterflies, bees, ladybirds, flies, gnats, and

THE LEGEND OF THE BULL STONES

many more whose names I didn't know. I yanked off my wool cloak, my Bronze Age garments, and my stinky sheepskin boots.

My cloak pin lay against my skin on its string round my neck, holding me together.

Barefoot in my sweat-drenched tee shirt and leggings, I looked up the hill at the Stones and raised my fist in satisfaction.

I was the Keeper, and the Stones had done what I wanted and let me into the time layer of the seventeenth century.

If ever I met that archaeologist again, she'd know what I was talking about, because now I'd made it happen. I'd created the legend that gave the Bull Stones their name, that Daniel had written about for a school essay. If I rescued him from the Long Mound.

I squinted at the sun. It was probably mid-afternoon. Five or six hours until dark, if it was late summer.

I led Free down the hill. If we were where I thought we were, I knew of a pond near the edge of the woods.

I found it where it still was in my time layer. It was bigger and cleaner here fed by a small spring. We both drank and I drenched myself in the cold sparkling water.

Picked off a dozen or so Bronze Age fleas.

As Free began to tear at the fresh grass and I laid my damp and dirty clothes out to bake in the sunshine, a distant cheer from the villagers reached me. Perhaps they'd started slaughtering the bulls. Smoke unfolded into the sky from some distant bonfire.

I lay in the sun, my cloak pin warm against my skin, and waited.

I was dreading going back to the Bronze Age. I wanted only

to return to my own time. But Keeper of the Stones or not, I was resigned to the knowledge that the Stones were probably going to take me back to the Bronze Age so I could finish what they'd started. The deep magic had its own rules. I could bend them, but I couldn't break them.

I'd return to my own time layer only when the Bullmaster was defeated, or die in a time layer that was not my own.

I'd intended travelling to the seventeenth century this time, and the Stones had made it happen so I could dispose of the bulls. But they'd taken me to steal the antibiotics Eothal needed from a time layer that was useless to me so I wasn't tempted to stay.

I picked a grass stem and sucked the sweet white end, lying back with the sun caressing my face. The only sounds were the buzz and whine of insects, the ripping of Free's teeth on the rich grass, and the birdsong in the woodland.

Would the Bullmaster, with his own magic, be able to force the Stones down the evil path he wanted? I thought it was possible.

I dozed until the sun moved enough for the trees to parasol me in shade.

As night approached, I recaptured Free and dressed in my Bronze Age clothing again, and we returned to the snow and the dark and the battle.

30

The Heart of the Battle

This time, I'd been gone longer than I expected. The Bronze Age battle had moved to the perimeter of the village. I rode beneath a high wild moon, its ghostly light falling on ground splotched with the dark sprawling shapes of dead and injured people and horses.

Howls and cries tore the dark, the clash of metal on metal clanging through the night. A dying horse gave a prolonged, heart-wrenching scream.

The kind face of Molasses leapt into my mind and panic crushed its way through me. What if he'd been taken for use as a battle horse and was injured or dead?

Free trembled beneath me as I turned her in the direction of the Long Mound.

I didn't dare look for the Bullmaster. I had to trust he was nowhere near the Mound. I was afraid that he might feel my search for him, however far off he was, and be drawn to me.

And now was my only chance. Free, refreshed from her afternoon of eating rich summer grass, was relieved to move along at a canter away from the battle zone, and we made straight for the Mound. My course took us within sight of beech and oak stands, and the old fear of wolves or boars settled in me when I wasn't thinking about the Bullmaster.

But in the end it wasn't any of those that caught up with us. It was Rugal, mounted on Sostis.

The red stallion was bathed in battle sweat and blood, black in the moonlight. Rugal had lost or discarded his cloak, and the moon struck flashes of light from the gold around his neck and wrists and from his sword.

'Still trying to save your brother, Lizzie?' he asked.

His tone mocked me. It was a challenge, a warning about the new ground between us. Free felt the adrenaline flare in my body and it made her jumpy.

'Still planning to help me, Rugal?' I asked lightly.

Despite the wind-blown drift of battle sounds, a silence fell on us. Where we were, it was just the soft footfalls of the horses, side by side in the rain-soaked meadowland.

The Long Mound lay ahead, secretive and closed beneath the low, cold sky.

'You cannot win,' Rugal said. 'Come with me and I will see that you are safe.'

His hand reached for mine, but I moved Free away.

'I arranged for the bulls to be killed,' I said, 'and they'll be killed.'

Rugal laughed, and when I urged Free to lengthen her stride, he moved his horse in step with mine.

'We do not need the bulls any longer,' he said.

He leant forward again, this time to take Free's rein and bring me under his control. His movement was so casual that I saw he regarded me not as Lizzie Brave but as Lizzie Greenwood, the Lizzie from my own time layer.

A follower.

But I carry fifty-pound sacks of feed at home on the farm, so I have muscles I know how to use. Rugal was riding bareback as always. No stirrups. What had he said?

If you wore those in battle it would be hard for your enemy to tip you off your horse. Perhaps I could tip him off his horse.

When he jammed Sostis against me again, I hooked my foot under his and flung my leg upward with every dreg of strength. To my astonishment, he went flying off the other side of the stallion.

Instantly I sent Free into a gallop. Sostis, with no rider to control him and a great liking for my mare, thought it was a race and took off with us.

We covered the distance to the Mound in a matter of seconds.

At the Endstones, I looked back. Rugal was nothing but a dark shape on the ground beneath the fragmented sky. I couldn't tell if he was moving or not.

I flung myself off Free and pulled the reins over her head so I could lead her. The stallion was taking a very personal interest in her and I gave him a tap across the nose with the reins. He backed off a few feet and stood with a surprised look on his handsome face.

The thaw meant the Endstone slabs were free of snow, and I forced my hand into the gap between them. Nothing.

I tried again, stretching to full height, jamming my hand so deep into the split that I tore skin off my fingers when I dragged them up between the slabs.

This time I found it, a thick lever of ice-cold metal. I gripped it and dragged it down hard, feeling the shooting pain of a fingernail tearing.

The lever moved down. As it moved, I got a better hold. I could feel it was attached to some kind of mechanism above the slabs. One of the Endstones rotated slowly, opening from the centre and turning sideways.

I stopped when the gap reached about eighteen inches.

I was facing a blackness so black that I didn't see how I could ever enter.

There was the sound of a heavy slap and Free broke from me and ran, the stallion with her. I whirled, knowing who I'd find.

Rugal stood there. His sword was in his hand, but his face was trying to conceal amazement.

'Lizzie Brave, do you ever give up?'

I slipped through the gap into the Mound and heaved the lever up hard, shutting him out. Shutting me in.

Now I was blind. And I was afraid of the dark.

The death-stench hit me like a wall.

It was the smell from that village. Mouldy, rotting, sickening. Sweat poured off me as I braced my hands against the rock, fighting the nausea. Despite the sweat, I felt too cold to move. Saliva flooded my mouth. I stopped breathing.

But I had to breathe, and at my next breath the death-stench thumped into me again.

Then it faded as I stood shuddering, head hanging between my arms, mouth open, sure I was going to throw up. Next breath, just the smell of plain earth. Next breath, same.

I stood panting until the cold, watery feeling left my bones and I could lift my head and open my eyes.

Not that it made any difference.

I put my hands tremulously on the Endstones, groping across them for the lever. I'd let go of it as the blackness clasped me. And now I couldn't find it, couldn't even find the join, though I hadn't moved since stepping through.

I didn't know if Rugal would try to follow. I was sure he'd know how to open the Endstones, but I thought he might just leave me here.

When I realised my right hand was wet, I touched it with my tongue and found that the wetness was blood. I traced the scores and cuts furrowed in my battle with the lever. Abruptly, my hand started throbbing.

Theseus had the sense to take a ball of string into his labyrinth to fight the Minotaur. I had nothing.

But this wasn't a labyrinth.

I turned until my back was against the Endstones and took sightless steps, my arms outstretched, walking into the lifeless heart of the Mound.

After a moment I called Daniel's name. My own voice nearly scared me to death, and I crept forward, not daring to speak again.

Then, instead of straining my eyes open uselessly, I closed them. The effect was instantaneous. I was choosing darkness, not letting darkness control me.

I kept each foot on the floor, sliding it over the earth, my hands out in front of me, my lower lip trapped between my teeth. Eyes closed.

Beside me, I felt a wall – earth and rock. I bumped one hand along its rough, cold surface as I advanced, invisible in the blackness.

Daniel used to have a puzzle, a shallow box that looked like a small block of wood and concealed a maze, with an opening at both ends. I fiddled with it a lot. You had to feed a marble through the maze without being able to see where it was rolling. Daniel got it as a stocking stuffer one Christmas, but it was me that became good at sending the marble through the hidden maze.

This was how I had to think of it. I had to be the marble in the maze.

I counted my steps, trying to lock them into my memory. From reaching out, I knew I was in a passageway with walls on either side. The passage was wide in most places, but now and then I could touch both walls by rocking from one foot to the other, fingertips outstretched sideways.

I found occasional spaces in the walls as I shuffled along. They seemed to be insets in the rock, and I did not want to feel around in them. Every pounding heartbeat reminded me the Mound was a multiple burial chamber.

Tirvold's ancestors were probably here. My ancestors too.

Right now, me too.

The darkness made the cold colder and it seeped into every part of me. As I stumbled along, arms out like a scarecrow, even my cloak couldn't trap whatever warmth I might have had. I assumed I still had feet inside my sheepskin boots, but I couldn't feel them. My teeth rattled with each breath.

But I kept my eyes closed and I kept going.

'Daniel,' I called.

My voice, in this dead voiceless place, shocked me into opening my eyes. Blackness. I closed them again. My breathing was erratic. I was afraid the smell would grab me again. The darkness was almost insignificant compared to that.

My outstretched foot bumped something on the ground, and my heart jolted so hard in my chest I almost fell.

After a moment, I cautiously tested the object with my foot. It was smaller than I expected, and lumpy. It rolled under the sole of my sheepskin boot. A thread of hope rose in me, a tiny flame, and I squatted. I groped through the dark and put my hand on the thing.

Recognition was so unexpected that for a moment, I couldn't take it in – smooth fabric, straps, buckles.

It was Daniel's backpack, still full of the things he'd stuffed in it in the light spilling from the refrigerator door. Food, a rain jacket. I'd watched him squeezing them in. Watched him cram the big torch into it as we stood on the doorstep in the moonlight.

I fumbled the buckles open and plunged a hand in. It closed on the familiar hard plastic and metal cylinder. Plastic! I'd almost forgotten what that was.

Dad's high-powered torch, practically a portable spotlight. I opened my eyes. My thumb found the switch and a huge beam of light blasted out.

It blinded me for a few seconds and then my eyes adjusted and I was able to see what surrounded me. The long, strong beam of light showed me a tunnel and earth walls, reinforced with rock in places. Having light was so overwhelming that for a whole minute I forgot why I was there.

Then I scooped up Daniel's backpack and shone the torch up the passage, exposing more earth and rock. Now that I was over the first gush of relief, I was afraid I'd see something much worse.

I straightened myself, kicking away the fear that I was already hopelessly lost in tunnels. Sealed in by the Endstones.

'Daniel!' I called again.

This time, my voice sounded strong.

Buoyed by the light, I screwed up the courage to investigate a burial chamber. Slow step by slow step, afraid it would be Daniel. Two men lay there, or their bones and clothes. Pots, weapons, and ornaments were arranged about their folded skeletons.

I stood looking for a while, and wondered how their lives had been. Took halting breaths in ancient musty air that smelled sweet and soft against the memory of the death-stench.

I left them in peace and moved deeper, further. I must be nearing the far end of the Mound. A wall was facing me. Against the wall, a heap, a shape.

I ran, stumbling behind the wavering beam of light.

Daniel.

My brother lay on his back on the earth floor, in the same position as the bones in the chambers. His skin was cold and dry, his eyes closed and flat.

But he was alive, somewhere deep inside, his breaths coming about one a minute. I shook him and yelled at him. No response. I pried his eyelids apart, but although he stirred a little, he didn't wake.

He was hibernating.

Anger churned in me so violently that I nearly hit him with the torch. I had no idea how long I'd been creeping about in this overgrown molehill. For all I knew the battle was over and the

Bullmaster had won.

I'd found Daniel, but I still had to save him. The little wooden puzzle had two openings for the marble, but the Mound only had one. If I couldn't wake him then somehow I had to drag him all the way back through the Mound to the Endstones.

Daniel was only a few inches taller than me, but he was heavier. I straightened him out, clamped the torch under my arm and hooked my hands under his armpits. I dragged him across the earth floor, grateful that I helped out on the farm and was strong from shifting feed sacks and hay bales. But it was hard going. He was floppy and keeping a good grip was a challenge.

About halfway along, I paused to rest for a few seconds. Daniel subsided on his back with his hands on his chest, imitating one of those carvings of knights on Medieval tombs. But he was still deeply asleep, far beyond my reach.

I turned him round so his feet were pointing in the direction I wanted to go. Stepping between his knees, I grasped his calves and picked up his legs. Dragging him in this wheelbarrow position was easier, though it meant the back of his head was bumping along the earth floor.

Maybe that would wake him up.

I dropped the torch. If it broke… I had to put down Daniel's legs to retrieve the torch. Kneeling, I shone the light on Daniel's sleeping face, pinched his cheeks.

'Daniel, wake up,' I said, 'I can't do this by myself.'

Struck by another thought, I turned him again, a half-turn this time. I began rolling him unevenly along. In places the passage narrowed and I had to jam his legs over, then half-lift his body, then follow up again with his legs.

Still Daniel showed no sign of waking. He remained clamped in his cold hibernation while sweat poured off me. But now the Endstones were in sight, at the limit of the torch beam.

I found a bottle of water in Daniel's backpack and drained it. I thought about leaving the bottle in one of the burial chambers. That would give the archaeologists something to think about.

But I tucked it away in the backpack instead, and was rewarded for not littering by finding half a bar of chocolate, which I scoffed hungrily. It was a long time since I'd eaten.

I didn't care about the dark anymore. And I wasn't lost.

We made it to the Endstones and I heaved Daniel against the wall in a sitting position. As he drooped, emitting a light snore now and then, I went to examine the stone slabs with the torch.

The joining point where they met was perfectly visible.

I slid my uninjured hand into the narrow gap and almost at once found the lever, up above my head at the limit of my reach.

Perhaps when I got Daniel outside into fresh air, he'd come out of his hibernation.

But as I grasped the lever, I found it was already moving.

Someone was opening the Endstones from the other side.

I ran back to Daniel, switching off the torch in some instinctive moment of self-preservation.

The Endstones scraped open, and battle cries and triumphant shouting burst in. Against a sky that was just beginning to pale with an arriving dawn, the Bullmaster's great horns curved.

He paused, and I was afraid he'd see or smell us. But he seemed injured. He stooped over, his breathing harsh and loud. He limped in without noticing us, and slammed the Endstones shut.

The Final Fight

Eothal must have driven the Bullmaster back to the Mound. I crouched in the blackness next to Daniel, listening to the Bullmaster's harsh panting. If we stayed absolutely quiet—meaning me, as Daniel had barely made a sound since I'd found him—perhaps he'd just stagger off somewhere and I'd be able to open the doors and we could escape.

I didn't give much for our chances if he found us, whether he was injured or not.

A loud thud sounded against the Endstones from the outside, and then another, and for a moment I thought the crowd of victors was trying to break in and finish off the Bullmaster.

That would have been fine. But with a stab of panic I realised it was much more likely they were bringing rocks to bury the Bullmaster inside forever.

My hand tightened on the torch, but I was careful to steer clear of the button. I didn't want the torch flashing on and alerting the Bullmaster to our presence.

Somehow I had to reach the lever again, open the Endstones and drag Daniel through, before the Horse People buried us too.

The Bullmaster stumbled off down the passage, completely at home in the dark. If he made it to the far end, he'd find that

Daniel was not where he'd left him.

In the Bullmaster's wake, the death-stench slugged me again with the cold nausea, the weakness, the fear. Everything else, it blocked out.

I dropped on all fours, almost puking, trying to make no sound, head pounding. Then it passed. My head cleared in cold waves. I groped beside me for Daniel, found him, and dragged his deadweight the last couple of metres to the Endstones. Once more, I propped him against the wall.

Another thud echoed through from the outside. Unless I got my act together it would be too late. The Endstones would be irreversibly blocked and we'd be sealed inside the tomb, until somebody in a time layer I hadn't found yet uncovered our bones.

I scrabbled one-handed for the lever, clutching the torch in the other, but not turning it on in case the light brought the Bullmaster. I slid my hand up inside the gap between the rock slabs. The Endstones didn't seem to be entirely closed. The gap was wider than it had been, and dim light showed between the slabs.

Just as I found the lever above my head, my arm stretched to the limit, and began to put my weight on it to yank it down, a vast screaming bellow slammed into me from the back of the Mound, the great roar of an enraged bull.

Daniel woke up and leapt to his feet in the dark, crashing into me and almost knocking me over.

'Bullmaster, I'm here!' he shouted.

I let go of the lever and grabbed at Daniel.

'Shut up!' I said, desperately.

What if my brother didn't know me? He certainly didn't

hear me.

'Bullmaster!' he shouted again. 'I await you!'

My reaching hand found his chest, and now I had my bearings I swung my arm back and whacked him, not sure what I'd land on in the dark. It was his face, a clean sharp slap that left my palm stinging.

'Daniel, it's me,' I said, 'Lizzie.'

His hands landed on my upper arms and he clutched them so hard it hurt.

'Lizzie?' he said. 'Lizzie?'

He sounded confused and afraid. I struggled free and put my arms round him, hugged his cold, unbending body.

'It's me,' I said. 'We've got to get out of here before the Bullmaster kills us.'

A thundering that sounded like hooves hammered through the Mound as the Bullmaster charged back for his prize. Even injured and limping, he still had speed and power.

In front of him came the death-stench.

The moment I felt the edge of it I took one last breath of clean air and let go of Daniel. I gripped the torch in both hands. He shuns daylight, Tirvold's voice said in my mind. I couldn't find the switch. Held the breath.

Held the breath.

Couldn't find the switch.

I had to breathe and sucked in the full-blown death-stench, felt my stomach hitting the back of my throat.

Then I found the switch and pinned the Bullmaster in the great beam of light.

His horned head was lowered to gore me, his shoulders caped

in bull-hide, his bellow ringing off the walls. I angled the light
so it speared him in the eyes. He halted and flung up his hands.
His left arm made that strange awkward gesture that he'd used
to direct the bulls, that had shadowed my dream.

The arm made of stone.

Daniel crouched on the floor, almost in a ball.

I realised I was going to die after all, and the realisation fu-
elled anger so strong that it drove out every other feeling in my
body: the smell, the nausea, the putrid cold that dragged at my
limbs, the fear. Fury took their place.

I gripped the torch with both hands, never shifting the high-
powered beam from the Bullmaster's eyes. I ran at him, powered
by fierce rage and bellowing myself.

He backed, awkward because of his injuries, lowering his
head to try to escape the light.

The death-stench faded again.

'You've lost,' I shouted. 'I killed your bulls, I'm taking my
brother back, and you're in here for ever.'

He was motionless, his wounds sinking him, and in the si-
lence I heard more thuds and scrapes from the other side of the
Endstones. Whether it was the torch or being the Keeper of the
Stones that gave me power to withstand him I didn't know. And
I didn't care. I'd had enough.

We had to get out. I backed up to Daniel again, the torch
beam locked on the Bullmaster. His face was hidden, the eyes
blank pits behind the slits in his helmet.

I reached down and shook Daniel's shoulder.

'Daniel, sit up,' I said. 'Hold the torch.'

Slowly, he raised himself. I wedged the torch into his hands, trying to ignore the rediscovery that they were deeply chilled.

'Don't take it off his eyes, not once, not for a second,' I said.

In the backlight from the beam, I found the join between the Endstones again and jammed my good hand in. The Endstones seemed to have shifted again—perhaps being pushed by the Horse People outside—and the lever had moved higher, almost out of my reach.

The Bullmaster crouched, weakened and bloodstained, impaled on the beam of light. Impaled on my will, my determination to free my brother.

I had the lever in my hand and tugged, but I couldn't move it.

'I tried to tell you that your way was wrong,' Daniel said.

His voice was distorted, like recorded speech running slow.

'Did the Bullmaster let you out?' I asked, in grunts.

I was tugging the immovable lever with increasing desperation. I'd have to get both hands on it somehow, use all my weight to shift it. I didn't need a conversation right now but I kept talking. Talking might be the only thing keeping Daniel awake and pointing the torch.

'No,' Daniel slurred. 'I dreamt it.'

'You found me,' I said, 'and I heard you, but I didn't understand.'

I jumped to get my other hand on the lever and try swing it down with my weight. It took Daniel by surprise and he dropped the torch. The light went out, and the Bullmaster sprang at us through the dark. I was already diving for the floor, groping for the torch, and the crash of stone against stone that should have been his arm crushing me sprayed us with chips and shards of broken rock.

I seized the torch. It was off, not broken. Daniel must have had his thumb on the button when he jumped. I snapped it on.

The Bullmaster gave a cry of pain as the light seared his eyes again, and flung up his one remaining hand. His other arm, the stone arm, lay in fragments by the Endstones.

I drove the light into his face and it sent him lurching away, down the passage.

With my free hand I grabbed the lever again. The huge blow from the Bullmaster had forced the Endstones ajar enough for me to get a grip on it and tug it down.

Morning sunshine poured in as the rock slabs grated open.

The gap wasn't much, but it was enough for Daniel and me to force ourselves through, and then the Horse People closed the Long Mound for the last time.

32

Shared Blood

Eothal was at the Mound, triumphant and bloodied from the battle. I stood before her with Daniel drooping beside me. We were both cold and shuddering. The rinsed yellow of the rising sun blinded me, as though being in the Mound had started to destroy my ability to live in daylight.

Squinting and so pale he was almost transparent, Daniel barely seemed alive.

Eothal commanded two of the Horse People to give up their mounts to Daniel and me, and we rode slowly back to the village with her. She shook her head, a little puzzled, when I asked if there had been a fire.

She had defeated the Bullmaster. Freed from the bulls, fully in command, Eothal had pitched her sword and her horse and her courage against him, driving him always towards the Mound. Sword to sword, she had wounded and disarmed him. As the battle went on, the men he'd overwhelmed switched sides and swelled the ranks of the Horse People.

With sunrise near, the Bullmaster finally surrendered and fled to the Long Mound.

As I listened to Eothal's account, it slowly sank in that the archaeologists wouldn't find evidence of battle and burning, and they wouldn't find my cloak pin. Those events, all that destruction, depended on me abandoning Daniel and going home to be an only child.

But I hadn't done that. I'd taken the bulls from the Bullmaster, and the Horse People had won.

Eothal was in her rightful place as Queen. The Bullmaster's power was broken and the captured villages freed.

Tonight, surely the Stones would take me and my brother back to our own time layer. Home.

I tried not to look at the bodies of men and horses on the trampled, bloodstained dregs of the snow. People were setting out with sledges in the cold morning light, to bring in the dead for funeral rites.

We trailed up the hill and into the village. Eothal rode in silence, her face a marble mask of sorrow. At the gate, she asked if I would go on alone with Daniel, and turned aside to talk to her people.

I longed to know what had happened to Free and Molasses but was afraid to ask.

The Horse People and their allies had already brought the injured into the village. The moans and cries from the huts followed us as our tired horses stumbled along the wooden walkways. A high, keening wail soared from some of the huts, the ones where death had struck.

We dismounted at Tirvold's hut and left the borrowed horses to find their own way to the pens. Tirvold was inside, eating, ashen with exhaustion but apparently unhurt.

He helped me with Daniel, who still so afflicted by the cold from the Mound that he was as twisted as an old man. Tirvold handed him a bowl of hot stew and he gulped it down. After a beaker of warm goat's milk for dessert, Daniel lay down on some wolfskins on the floor. By the time I'd covered him with a horse blanket, he was asleep.

A real sleep, not the dark hibernation of the Mound.

As I ate a second bowl of hot lamb stew and drank a beaker of goat's milk myself, the best thing I ever tasted in my life, I asked where Rugal was.

Tirvold stared at the floor.

'We met in battle,' Tirvold said. 'I was beside Eothal, and he was beside the Bullmaster. I had to kill him.'

I'd known something like this would be the answer, but it was still a massive shock and I stopped eating for a moment, my eyes burning. Tirvold was quiet. Then he touched the back of my hand.

I met his gaze. Grey circles had stamped themselves around his blue eyes, eyes so like Daniel's that I glanced across to make sure my brother was still asleep on the floor.

'There is something I must tell you,' Tirvold said, so quietly I could hardly hear him. 'I did intend Daniel to be taken by the Bullmaster, because he looked so like me and I needed time.'

I set down my empty stew bowl.

'Rugal told me,' I said. 'I didn't want to believe him.'

'Rugal knew,' Tirvold said. 'When we went on the boar hunt, I believed he would tell the Bullmaster, and the Bullmaster would try to take me once evening fell. That is how Rugal knew I planned that Daniel would be taken instead, but he could not give you that proof without betraying himself.'

I didn't say anything, and Tirvold sighed.

'I needed some time,' he said again. 'To help Eothal. I hope you can forgive me.'

'I can,' I said. 'Everything worked out fine. And you're family.'

I couldn't help grinning. The wary expression fell from Tirvold's face and a tired smile lit it instead.

'But surely, even if the Bullmaster didn't realise it, Rugal must have told him Daniel wasn't you?' I asked.

'Rugal believed Daniel knew how to wield the power of the Stone Circles,' Tirvold said. 'So it still bought me time, because they thought he would reveal it.'

There was no way I could be angry with Tirvold. After all, I'd been ready to leave my brother behind in the Bronze Age to save my own skin. I couldn't blame Tirvold for doing almost the same thing.

'I was wrong about the Stones,' Tirvold said.

'How?' I asked.

'I thought they had taken me to your time because of Daniel, because he looked like me and I could use him to trick the Bullmaster. But it was you, another Keeper of the Stones, that we needed.'

His eyebrows came together as he considered the chain of events.

'Though I suppose if Daniel had not been taken, you would not have done everything you did,' he said. 'So it is all entwined.'

'I'm glad the Stones brought us here,' I said. 'If they hadn't, I might not exist. If that makes any sense at all.'

Tirvold held out his hand, and I put mine in it. He turned it over gently, examining the cuts and scrapes and my swollen knuckles.

'I did not look to find such courage in anyone,' he said. 'I hope you are indeed my descendant, a child of the Horse People's blood. Nothing gives me more honour.'

I couldn't think of anything to say. He was only a couple of years older than me. It was incredible to think of him as my ancestor. Already dead for three thousand years in my time layer, so vivid and strong in his own.

'Daniel will recover soon,' Tirvold said. 'If you take him back to your time, it will restore him.'

33

The Right Time

In the evening, we took Free and Molasses unscathed from the horse pen. Daniel had slept all day. He was warm and his voice was back to normal, but his movements were still a little stiff.

I kept my cloak pin round my neck. I wanted to remember.

It was surprisingly hard to leave, knowing this would be the last time. But in the Stone Circles, I led us through from the Bronze Age time layer into our own.

This time, it really was our own. We were back at midnight on the cold solstice night that started it all.

In front of us, our tracks marched up the hill in the snow, churned all over by the tracks of the vanished bulls. This was the view we'd had in the moments before we first crossed from our own time layer, except Tirvold was no longer with us.

We were alone under the starry winter sky, and in the weary silence that comes at the end of a long journey, we rode home.

❧❧❧❧❧❧❧

As we settled the horses in the barn with blankets and hay, Daniel stretched as though he were finally waking up.

'Now we know how to use the Bull Stones, we should do it again,' he said.

'I didn't realise you had such a good time,' I said sarcastically.

'Well, maybe next time I would,' he said.

I thought Daniel would forget, the way I had without my cloak pin — but he'd brought his own Bronze Age memory ticket.

In the kitchen, he switched on a light, opened his backpack, and pulled out a pottery bowl, imprinted around the edges with cord impressions. He turned it slowly in his hands, an amazed half-smile on his face.

'Look at this,' he said. 'I took it from Tirvold and Eothal's hut. I own probably the only perfect piece of Bronze Age pottery in the country. What a start for an aspiring archaeologist.'

'Nobody will ever believe you,' I said.

'Yeah, you're probably right,' he said. 'But I know that one of the great queens of the Bronze Age ate out of it.'

'She's been dead for three thousand years,' I said flatly.

I tried to sound as though that was the end of it, but it was almost impossible to grasp that all those people I'd met, people whose lives were still fresh in my mind, were long turned to dust in the land around me.

'That's where the Bull Stones come in,' Daniel said.

I glanced at the kitchen clock. It was almost two in the morning. I was exhausted. But I had to know one thing.

'Do you know how to use the Stones?' I said. Daniel frowned.

'Actually, no,' he said. 'I'd need your help.'

Good, I thought. Only I knew the secret.

I was almost too tired to take off my boots. My hands throbbed. The cuts and bruises on them were going to take some explaining, if Mum or Dad noticed.

'I'm going to bed,' I said.

ↄ_ↄ ↄ_ↄ ↄ_ↄ ↄ_ↄ ↄ_ↄ ↄ_ↄ

The day after Christmas Day, Mum and Dad drove into the village for somebody's Boxing Day lunch. Daniel got a lift with them. He was meeting up with friends.

After the others left, I saddled Free and rode to the Bull Stones.

I'd found a thin necklace chain and now wore my cloak pin on it around my neck, under my clothes, next to my skin where it kept my memory working. I'd vowed privately that I'd never take it off.

Daniel had put his Bronze Age bowl on his bedroom windowsill and he'd already forgotten how he came by it. He thought he'd found it on the dig in the summer. If he picked it up he might remember, but I wasn't sure he would.

ↄ_ↄ ↄ_ↄ ↄ_ↄ ↄ_ↄ ↄ_ↄ ↄ_ↄ

The weather had warmed in the past couple of days and most of the snow had melted, leaving pressed grass and wet ground. There was no sign the bulls had ever been there, chasing us with Tirvold through the Stones. No sign that Tirvold had ever existed.

Near the centre of the Bull Stones, I dismounted and placed my palm flat on the rough cold surface of the Moonstone. Disappointment trickled through me as I felt nothing but cold, unyielding rock beneath my hand.

Then it started, deep in the heart of the Stone. The vibration, the humming that told me the Bull Stones remembered me and recognised me for who I was.

They knew me, and I smiled. I was the Keeper of the Stones.

About the Illustrator

Kelsea Rothaus is a Pacific Northwest based American illustrator and designer most known for her ink wash technique and digital illustration.

With her tools for artistic expression, love of nature, and rock music, Kelsea dives into projects while on-the-go with her dog, Apollo. She creates with an appreciation for juxtaposition of light and dark – gravitating towards shadowy and whimsical themes that incorporate wildlife, musical or literary references.

About the Author

When Roz Kay was eight years old, she visited Stonehenge. At that time it wasn't fenced off and you could walk about among the huge stones and touch them. She never forgot the feel of those ancient stones beneath her hand. So, years later when she wrote this book, the story began with another stone circle.

Roz is a published short story writer and has been a radio and newspaper journalist. She's an animal lover and has had horses, dogs, cats, rabbits, guinea pigs, birds, and many more creatures. While growing up, Roz lived in Ghana, Canada, and Sabah as well as the UK. She's also lived in the US. She loves books, theatre, history, art, travel, wildlife, and sports.

Roz now lives in England with two greyhounds called Lyra and Fletcher, close to the great stone circles at Stonehenge and Avebury in Wiltshire. She's working on a sequel to *The Keeper of the Stones*. Roz would love to hear from you if you enjoyed *The Keeper of the Stones* – please email Roz care of: books@hayloft.eu

Acknowledgements

Many years have gone into the writing of this story, and numerous friends and family members have helped me along the way. The first writer's group I joined saw early drafts of this novel and gave me thoughtful and encouraging comments: you know who you are. When I was a teenager (and already writing what became an element of this story) my English teacher Colin Carter inspired me and always pushed me to do better—thank you. My children, Josie and Nathaniel, are kind and supportive about anything I write and that means everything. Grateful thanks go to Pat Marshall and Lisa Taylor, who have willingly read drafts of various things I've written and given me candid and helpful feedback. I'm incredibly grateful to Kelsea Rothaus for agreeing to illustrate this book and by doing so elevating it to a different level. Most of all, thank you to Dawn Robertson, my editor and publisher, for taking a chance on *The Keeper of the Stones.*